"It's exciting to mak[e] someone you don't know.

Matt's words thrilled Molly even as she protested. "But that doesn't work for marriage. An oversexed couple who meet at a singles' bar and get married a week later don't stand a chance. Your sister and her fiancé have the perfect formula for a happy marriage—they know and respect each other."

"So you measure happiness by familiarity rather than intensity? That's a boring concept, Prescott. It sounds to me like you have something against sex."

He was getting to her and, what was worse, he seemed to be enjoying it. "I'm not talking about sex," she said, flustered. "I don't care about that."

"You don't care about sex? Why, Prescott, you must really lead a boring life." His mouth quirked into the beginning of a smile.

"We're talking about your sister's wedding. Don't try to distract me," she warned. "And if you're planning sabotage, I'll—I'll . . ."

"Call the wedding police?" Matt laughed, but his eyes challenged her. "I'll do whatever's necessary to see that the wedding doesn't happen."

The **Madeline Harper** writing team proves that two heads are better than one. Madeline Porter and Shannon Harper met in college and, after years of friendship, decided to merge their passion for writing. At the time, Madeline was living in Colorado, the setting for their latest Temptation, *Wedding Bell Blues*. Why did they choose to write on the topic of holy matrimony? "We wanted to show all the hysteria and crises that lead up to putting on a fancy wedding." Readers should have a lot of fun with this comedy of errors. Just be thankful it's not *your* wedding!

Books by Madeline Harper

HARLEQUIN TEMPTATION

WEDDING BELL BLUES

MADELINE HARPER

Harlequin Books

TORONTO • NEW YORK • LONDON
AMSTERDAM • PARIS • SYDNEY • HAMBURG
STOCKHOLM • ATHENS • TOKYO • MILAN
MADRID • WARSAW • BUDAPEST • AUCKLAND

To Birgit, with thanks for ten years of Temptation

Published June 1993

ISBN 0-373-25547-0

WEDDING BELL BLUES

1

MATTHEW KINCAID OPENED the car door and planted his hiking boots firmly in the six inches of powdery snow. He looked up at the pale gray Victorian house that towered above him, with its bright blue shutters, gleaming white porch and balustrades. The house where he'd grown up, the house he always returned to. No matter where he traveled—across continents or over oceans—it was always good to come home.

His life was filled with adventure, even danger, and it was exactly the way he wanted it. But as he walked up the old path, bordered by ageless elm trees, he experienced a sense of timelessness and serenity that was steadfast in an ever-changing world.

He left deep footprints in the freshly fallen March snow as he approached the house and climbed the steps to the wide porch. Key in hand, he unlocked the door and stepped into the hall. At six-thirty in the morning the sun had just come up over the plains, but the house was still dark. He flicked on a light.

"Hey, Krista, get yourself out of bed. I'm home and I want to see my little sister." Matt waited at the bottom of the wide staircase, then called again. "You can sleep another time, Kristabel. Wake up!"

"Matt . . . oh, Matt. . . ." His sister appeared on the landing, tying the sash of her flannel robe. "I can't believe you're back!" She flew down the stairs and flung herself into her brother's arms.

Matt swung her around in a huge circle. "Just like when we were kids, eh, Krista?"

Krista fell back against the balustrade, trying to catch her breath. "And you still knock the wind out of me—just like when we were kids!" She pushed her blond hair out of her eyes and smiled up at her brother. "So one of my telegrams must have finally caught up with you."

"Telegrams?" Matt shrugged out of his jacket and tossed it on a hall chair. "I didn't get any telegrams. What's wrong? Is the store—"

"It's in great shape, still the best mountaineering shop west of the Mississippi. And I'm still the best manager."

"I know that," he affirmed. "Now, come on." He slipped his arm around her waist. "You're all right, and the store's all right so you can tell me about those telegrams over coffee."

"How about coffee and eggs and pancakes and sausage?" Krista asked with a grin. "Doesn't that sound better?"

"Sounds like heaven to a man whose meals for the past two months have consisted mostly of beef jerky and tea, consumed over a campfire that really did nothing to ward off the cold."

"So if you didn't get my telegrams, why're you home?" Krista asked. She took out the eggs and sausage while Matt began filling the coffeepot. "Problems with K2?"

"K2, my dear sister, is a hell of a lot tougher than its sister, Mount Everest."

"I can't imagine you'd think any mountain in the Himalayas would be easy."

"I don't." Matt measured the coffee grounds to ensure the brew would be strong and black enough to suit his tastes. "But it may have at least been manageable if it weren't for the damned blizzard that shut us down for ten days. Then one of my climbing mates got pneumonia, our guide broke his leg . . . Hell, even I know when to give up."

"Give up?" Krista fixed him with a cool gaze that people had said was so like his own. "We Kincaids don't ever give up."

Matt laughed. "Then let's say back off for a while. We're forming a new expedition to go out this fall. We'll make it then." He took two mugs from the cabinet and set them on the counter. Then he leaned back, crossed his arms and asked, "So if nothing's wrong, why did you want to get in touch with me?"

He smiled at his sister. "You got accepted at grad school. You're going to make your brother proud and get yourself out of Dillard into the big, bad world."

Krista turned away from the sausage sizzling in the pan. The look on her face was one she'd often worn when she was a little girl and had something to confess.

"All right. It's not grad school. Then what is it?"

The look was almost apologetic.

"I have a terrible feeling I'm not going to like this," Matt said.

"I hope you are, Matt. The fact is, I'm getting married. Brent and I are getting married."

"Oh, that." Matt let out a long sigh. "You and Brent. Honey, you two have been getting married since...hell, since high school."

"Seventh grade, actually," Krista corrected as she turned back to the stove. "That's when we started going steady." She neatly flipped the sausages onto a paper towel, then faced her brother again. "It's true this time, Matt. We're getting married this month."

"Do you—have to?" Matt asked through dry lips.

"Have to? Matt, that's such an old-fashioned question."

"What's the old-fashioned answer, Krista?"

"Well, kinda," she said with a laugh.

"This isn't funny. At least not to me."

"All right." She broke a few eggs into a bowl and looked back at him with a grin. "I'm not pregnant, if that's what you mean." She stirred the eggs vigorously. "But I still have to get married—"

"Krista—" Matt's voice conveyed his irritation.

"Because I won the Wedding of the Month, an absolutely wonderful, splendiferous, fabulous, earth-shattering June wedding. And I won!"

Matt relaxed slightly. He'd have time between now and June to help Krista change her mind and to push for grad school. "June? So it's not March after all."

"It's a June wedding, but we're getting married in March." At Matt's warning look, Krista defended her remark quickly. "Magazines call it 'lead time.' Brent and I will be the Wedding of the Month for June, but the wedding has to be photographed in March. So in a few days, Molly will be flying out—"

"Molly? Who the hell is Molly?" Since the coffee was now ready, Matt filled his mug. A shot of brandy in it might offset the shock of Krista's news but he decided he needed to keep a clear head.

"Molly Prescott. She's my editor. Or at least she's the editor for the Wedding of the Month at *Wedding* magazine."

"*Wedding* magazine," Matt repeated with wonder. "You mean there's a magazine just for people who're getting married?"

"There're several," Krista said airily, "but *Wedding* is the best."

"When this Prescott woman arrives, what exactly will she do?"

"Oh, she'll make arrangements," Krista explained. "Like helping me choose my dress, order flowers, decorate the house.... We're having the ceremony here. You don't mind, do you, Matt?"

2

MOLLY PRESCOTT TOOK a final look through the folder on her desk and nodded with satisfaction. "This time we have a winner, Jeri," she said.

Molly's assistant handed over her itinerary, her airline ticket to Denver and a second file. "No doubt about it, boss. Krista's a knockout, the groom has all-American good looks, the house is Victorian with lots of curlicues and a grand staircase. I can just see the bride sweeping down those stairs! What a photo opportunity." Jeri paused briefly before adding, "And then, of course, there's the brother."

"Oh, yes. He'll give the bride away."

"That's the one possible glitch," Jeri said. "We may need a stand-in, just in case Matt doesn't make it in time."

"Wait a minute." Molly frowned as she sat back in her desk chair. "I want everything settled before I get on that plane, Jeri. I thought the brother had been contacted."

"We've sent wires. So has Krista. He's difficult to get hold of."

"Jeri, this is *Wedding* magazine, and we're living in the 1990s. Send the man a fax."

Jeri started to laugh but stopped when she saw her senior editor's expression. "Do you know who the brother is?"

"Of course." Molly checked the file. "His name's Matt. Matt Kincaid."

"I just put another folder on your desk, Molly, information they put together down in research. Maybe you should look through it."

Molly flipped it open and sifted through the papers. She stopped at a tear sheet from the cover of a sports magazine. "Is this him?"

"That's our man. *The* Matt Kincaid."

Molly shook her head. "Doesn't ring a bell."

"That shows how much you know about macho stuff, Molly. He's only one of the most famous mountain climbers in the world. Check out that photo. It's the cover of *Outdoor Man* magazine."

"I don't know anything about *Outdoor Man*, and all I know about the outdoors is that it gives me hay fever."

"Wildflowers give you hay fever," Jeri corrected.

"But remember, wildflowers grow outdoors."

"All right, all right," Jeri acquiesced. She nodded toward the photo. "Matt Kincaid is a famous mountain climber. The *most* famous. He climbs every mountain worth climbing, then gets feted by the jet set and ends up on a yacht anchored off some Caribbean island, dancing with beautiful socialites 'til the wee small hours of the morning...."

"Jeri, I get the picture. You're romanticizing again."

"Of course, I am. I'm a romantic. I'm in love with love. That's why I work for *Wedding* magazine."

Molly sipped her coffee thoughtfully. "I'm surprised you haven't become disillusioned. Take for example last June's couple of the month. They filed for divorce in December. And the October couple, who married in that quaint seaside town in Maine, got an annulment. An annulment! I ask you, is that even possible in this day and age?"

"I still believe in happily ever after."

"I don't understand," Molly said as she rose from her chair. She began to pace in front of the floor-to-ceiling windows that overlooked Manhattan. "These couples take all the time and trouble to enter our contest, to write to *Wedding* and convince us how much they love each other and why they should win the Wedding of the Month and then . . . and then . . ."

Jeri threw back her head and laughed. "And then they have the audacity not to stay married. There oughtta be a law."

Molly stopped her pacing and frowned. "You take this much too lightly, Jeri. It's serious business."

Jeri bit back more laughter. "If you say so, Molly, although some of us think you should take other people's weddings less seriously and think about one of your own."

"'Some of us' meaning you," Molly shot back.

"Well . . ."

"And who do you suggest I marry? Well, let me tell you the kind of men who are available in New York—they're either power-hungry workaholics, neurotics or wimps. And on the outside chance that any one of these fabulous prospects was interested in romance at all, it would be nothing more than a one-night stand."

"You're so cynical, Molly."

"You call it cynical. I call it realistic."

"'Course, there're other places for romance besides New York."

Molly heaved a sigh. "You're thinking perhaps of Colorado?"

"Perhaps. Take a look at the cover photo, Molly. He's a real hunk."

"I hate that expression," Molly murmured as she glanced again at the photograph. Matthew Kincaid *was* handsome, with a strong face, cool measuring gray eyes, a straight, masculine nose and high cheekbones. In the picture, he wore a parka with a fur-lined hood, but a strand of hair straggled across his forehead. It was light brown, streaked with gold. His mouth was hidden by a beard. No big surprise, Molly thought. All the so-called macho men these days seemed to have beards.

"I don't like beards," she said.

"No problem. Dig a little deeper."

Molly shuffled through the pictures and found a more recent photo of a clean-shaven Matt Kincaid. The accompanying article named him one of America's most eligible bachelors. Molly checked the date. Two years ago. "He was twenty-nine then, which makes him—"

"Thirty-one and still eligible."

"I get the drift, Jeri, and I appreciate the thought, but I'm not looking for a fling in the mountains with a macho hunk." She glanced at the picture again. "He probably thinks he's God's gift to women, anyway. So thanks, but no thanks."

"Keep looking," Jeri suggested.

He was certainly more handsome without the beard, Molly conceded. His chin was firm, and although his mouth was strong there was a sensual fullness to his lower lip.

Molly put the folder aside, hoping that the gesture didn't appear as reluctant as it was. "I'll be in Dillard for only one reason—to concentrate on a fabulous June wedding for Krista and her fiancé, Brent Oliver. You know, they've been sweethearts since the seventh grade. As far as I'm concerned, that's what true love is all about—stability, longevity, and a quiet harmony." She smiled broadly. "Perfect, at last."

"Perfect, if a little boring," Jeri qualified. Seeing Molly's frown, she added, "But I'm sure you're right. They certainly have longevity going for them—Brent and Krista have dated for years. They have everything in common—same goals, same hobbies, same friends. And listen to this, Brent says in the questionnaire that his mother adores Krista. It's more than perfect—it's too good to be true."

"I'm betting everything on this one, Jeri. Finally, I'm covering a marriage that will last. Maybe in ten years or so—" she smiled and continued "—when I'm editor-in-chief—I'll stage a second wedding for them in our anniversary issue."

"I don't have the slightest doubt that you'll be editor-in-chief, and probably in less than ten years. And maybe you're right—maybe we'll revisit Krista and Brent when they're an old married couple with kids."

"I'm already looking forward to it. For a change I'm not dealing with flakes—people who fell in love while skydiving, or met on a three-day cruise, or found instant karma in their meditation class. Krista and Brent are different—these two are magic. They're what great weddings are made of. This isn't the Wedding of the Month. Trust me, it's the Wedding of the Year." Molly glanced down at the file and caught another glimpse of Matt Kincaid's photo. His eyes, which she had considered cool and measuring, now seemed skeptical and cynical, staring challengingly into hers.

Deliberately she closed the file on his face, determined to put him out of her mind.

Jeri was resistant to that idea. "Don't dismiss him so summarily," she suggested.

"Sorry, but he's not my type."

"Just trying—"

"I appreciate the thought, Jeri, but I'm afraid Matt Kincaid and I are going to be like ships that pass in the night. Once he's gotten his sister down the aisle, he'll be history, assuming he's even there."

"Something tells me he'll be there."

"If not, we'll just find a replacement, a cousin or uncle, or—" Molly paused, thoughtful. "No, that won't work. If I remember correctly from Krista's application, she has no close relative...."

"Just her brother. Their parents were killed in an airplane accident several years ago, and there aren't any uncles, aunts or cousins. Only Matt. Obviously, he and Krista are very close. So don't worry. He'll show."

"Hmm." Molly wasn't quite sure whether that was a plus or a minus. Protective siblings, especially heroic older brothers, could be more trouble than they were worth.

MOLLY WENT OVER her notes on the plane. Jeri had everything organized. To be sure that Dillard would look like June in March, she'd found someone to bring a snowblower to the Kincaid house the morning of the wedding to clear off the snowy residue. Florists had been hired to fill the house—and the yard—with hothouse flowers that had been forced into bloom.

That left the most important ingredient—the photographer. For assignments like this, Molly chose from a very short list of professionals who could combine immense talent with an ability to get along with people in every social strata. Only a handful of staff and freelance photographers met Molly's stringent requirements.

She stretched out, reclined her seat to a comfortable position and opened the file. She found that on this assignment she'd bottomed out with her fourth choice. Technically the most proficient, Pete Walenski was charming, agreeable and never acted like a prima donna. There was just one problem. He was incredibly attractive and all the women—from the mother of the bride, through the bridesmaids, right up to the bride herself—were fair game for Pete's charm. *Well, let him flirt*, Molly decided. The bride was too much in love to succumb, and she was really the only one who mattered. Besides, his pictures would be fabulous.

Snow for a June wedding, a flirtatious photographer, and possibly a missing brother—those were her only problems, and they were offset by the certainty that the Kincaid–Oliver wedding was going to be the most exciting, the most beautiful and the most successful to date. This wedding would prove that Molly's monthly feature put the magazine head and shoulders above others in the field and made her the hottest editor out there. In a few years, she hoped to be running the whole show. Success felt good, she decided as she reached for the tiny pillow, fluffed it as much as possible, jammed it between her seat and the armrest, and settled down for a bumpy trip between New York and Denver. With an unwelcome stopover in Chicago, it was going to be a long flight. But the couple at the end of the line would make it all worthwhile. Krista and Brent would be at the airport to meet her. Molly couldn't wait to see her perfect couple.

SHE WAS THE LAST passenger off the plane at Stapleton International Airport in Denver, and she felt about as fresh as the various pillows she'd manhandled since leaving New York. An unexpected snowstorm had held up flights from Chicago and after waiting half the night she'd opted for a connection to Denver via Dallas. At each step along the way, she'd called the Kincaid house with updates and received assurances from Krista not to worry, she'd be met.

But as Molly struggled with her carry-on luggage past the security checkpoints and searched through the faces in the crowd, there was no sign of Krista or Brent. She knew that she'd recognize them immediately from the numerous photographs. After all, they were her dream couple.

But where the hell were they?

Molly reached a relatively uncrowded corner that was out of the way of the traffic flow, dropped her bags and cursed to herself. What if there'd been a confusion about the messages, or a delay, or an accident? Her mind went through all the possibilities and none was encouraging. She was too tired to search out a rental car company and make the trip alone to Dillard, but she wasn't about to spend any more time in an airport. A long row of pay phones lined the wall; she made her way toward them.

Then she saw him, leaning casually against the railing. He was long and lean and wore skintight jeans, cowboy boots, a leather jacket and a Stetson. Molly looked again. Cool gray eyes, high cheekbones, straight nose. Krista had sent her brother to meet the plane.

And Jeri was right. Even in her exhaustion, Molly could tell he was a hunk. There was no other way to describe the tall muscular man who was waiting for her.

Dragging her luggage behind, Molly approached Matt Kincaid. When she stopped a few feet from him, he looked at her, puzzlement in his eyes.

"Mr. Kincaid, that is if you are Matt Kincaid, I'm Molly Prescott. From *Wedding* magazine." She released her bags, stepped forward and stuck out her hand.

Slowly he extended his own hand. "Well, who would have figured it," he said drolly. "I thought you'd be . . . well, older and more . . . well, just older."

"And taller." Molly pulled herself to her full height of five feet three inches and ran her fingers through her hair, which had come unpinned and straggled around her face and neck. *And more sophisticated.* That's what he'd meant, but hadn't said—and she certainly wasn't going to! But Molly knew it. Her long wool skirt was rumpled; her makeup was practically nonexistent after so many hours. She hadn't bothered to take it off and start over in the middle of the night. All in all, she wasn't the image of the well-dressed New York editor, and she was irritated that he'd noticed.

"I'm sure you make up in smarts for what you lack in size," Matt commented lazily.

Not bothering to respond to that assumption, Molly asked, "Wasn't Krista planning to meet me?" She might as well let him know from the outset that Krista and Brent were the reason she was here—and no one else.

"I talked her out of it."

"Oh? Why?" Molly persisted.

"Because we need to discuss a few things. We can do it over coffee while we wait for your luggage."

"This *is* my luggage," Molly said, indicating her two pieces of carryon. "I travel light."

A momentary flicker of admiration crossed Matt's face. Molly imagined that he was a man who traveled light, too. Score one for Molly's side, she thought.

"Okay. We'll have coffee anyway."

Molly was nonplussed. He hadn't even bothered to ask her opinion. Well, she was tired and she wanted to get to her final destination, not sit around in another airport. "Couldn't we talk as we drive? I've really seen enough of airports for a while."

"Umm, we could." Matt slung one of her bags over his shoulder and picked up the other. Then with his free hand, he steered Molly down the concourse. "But I think we'll talk here."

Molly knew two things at that moment. Matt Kincaid was used to getting his own way, and something was wrong with the wedding plans. Obviously that was what he wanted to talk about.

"All right," she relented. "But I'd like more than just coffee. I'd like a full breakfast. Airplane food doesn't appeal to me very much, and somehow on this trip it was worse than ever."

"A full breakfast, it is," Matt agreed. "I sure don't want you getting back on the plane hungry."

"Back on the plane? What in the world are you talking about?" Even though Matt was carrying her bags, he took long strides, forcing Molly to almost run to keep up with him. "I'll be here until after the wedding, Mr. Kincaid."

"Yeah, well, that's what we need to talk about."

Molly took a few quick steps and caught up again. "What do you mean?"

"I mean there's not going to be a wedding."

3

MOLLY ALLOWED HERSELF to be led into the airport coffee shop. She remained silent, curbing her reaction to his remark. She'd already decided it was wishful thinking on the part of an overly protective brother who spent too much time climbing mountains. What in the world could he know about what was right for Krista and Brent? First she'd let him explain. *Then* she'd react.

They settled in a booth and gave the waitress their orders. Suddenly Molly didn't feel hungry at all, but after her earlier ultimatum, she was determined to stick with a full breakfast. She ordered eggs, bacon, toast, hash browns, coffee and orange juice, and told herself that somehow she'd manage to eat it all.

When they were alone, Matt looked at her with what Molly decided was his conciliatory gaze. "I'm sure you'll understand my decision about the wedding. You're an intelligent woman. Besides being a very beautiful one."

"You don't know anything about me, Mr. Kincaid," Molly responded, "least of all my degree of intelligence."

"You're a senior editor at a national magazine that ranks pretty high in its field, or so I'm told. You're very young to hold that position, so you must be bright. It figures. I'd expected that, but I'd also expected someone cold, businesslike and tough as nails. That you're not."

The waitress brought their coffee, and Molly gulped down half of hers, hoping it would stimulate her for what lay ahead. "How do you know I'm not cold and businesslike? And tough as nails?"

"With that face? With those big brown eyes and that curly hair? Never. You look more like you could be a friend of Krista's. Not a powerful, big-time, hard-driving editor, who won't listen to reason."

Molly tried to keep her voice calm. "Mr. Kincaid—"

"Matt," he corrected.

"I think I'll address you formally, and as soon as you hear what I have to say, I'm sure you'll want me to continue calling you Mr. Kincaid."

"Never."

"I see your game plan, Mr. Kincaid. If I were sweet and understanding the way you think I am, then you could just take a few minutes of your time, buy me breakfast, explain why you don't want your sister's wedding in our magazine, and put me back on the plane. Right?"

Matt found himself smiling. "Well, not exactly."

"But something like that. By buttering me up and flattering me, you thought I'd go soft. But the truth is, you've misjudged me. I'm actually a tough, businesslike editor. My looks belie my personality." She tossed her head. " So, now what's your game plan, Mr. Kincaid? And don't patronize me."

Matt actually laughed out loud. "Well, Ms. Prescott . . . Or maybe I'll just call you Prescott. It has a certain ring to it."

"Suit yourself." Molly drank the rest of her coffee.

"I didn't intend to be patronizing. In fact, I meant just what I said. Big brown eyes are still big brown eyes even if they belong to a tough editor."

He smiled again broadly, and Molly realized that her first impression when she saw the picture on *Outdoor Man* magazine had been right. Matthew Kincaid thought he was God's gift to women.

"I'm just a plain man who speaks from his heart," he added.

"Sure, sure," Molly muttered, "and Napoleon was just an ordinary French soldier. Now, why don't you want Krista's wedding in my magazine? Is it the publicity that bothers you?"

"Not at all. It's the wedding that bothers me, this wedding that you and Krista have concocted. It should never take place."

Molly's breakfast arrived just as her appetite returned. She'd been right. This had nothing to do with Krista and Brent and everything to do with a protective older brother. Molly carefully buttered her toast, took a big bite, then looked up at Matt.

He was waiting. For the first time since they entered the coffee shop, Molly let herself observe Krista's brother, her nemesis. His hair was definitely more blond than brown, his eyes appeared more blue than gray and, unbelievably, he was more handsome in person than in his photo. The waitress hadn't been able to take her eyes off him. Well, Molly could handle him.

"I didn't concoct anything," she denied. "Your sister entered our Wedding of the Month contest of her own free will."

"And you pushed her with your steamroller tactics."

"Steamroller tactics!" Molly couldn't keep the amazement from her voice.

"All the promises you've made her. Big wedding, beautiful dress, exotic flowers, perfect—well, perfect everything. She told me all about it, Prescott. What young girl wouldn't have her head turned? You're pressuring her, and I want you to back off."

Molly almost smiled. He was no longer saying there'd be no wedding. He'd backed down, but she wasn't backing off.

"This is your sister's wedding, and she's the one who should make the decisions. I talked to her—" Molly checked her watch "—less than ten hours ago, and she was more excited than ever, and certainly just as committed to her decision. Let her run her own life, Mr. Kincaid. What makes you think this is any of your business, anyway?"

"Because she's my little sister."

"She's twenty-three years old! Maybe she was your little sister ten years ago. But she's a woman now."

"Whatever her age, I love her and I want the best for her."

Molly eagerly attacked her bacon. "So it's best for her not to get married?"

"Exactly. She shouldn't be getting married to anyone yet—certainly not to Brent."

"Brent seems like a fine young man."

"And what do you base that assumption on?"

"Mr. Kincaid, the questionnaires our applicants fill out are very thorough. Brent's indicates that he's a caring person. He's smart and ambitious—"

"And he plays a hell of a game of tennis and skis like a pro. He's honest and determined and very charming."

Molly relaxed. This was getting easy.

"But Krista has dated him since the seventh grade. She's never known any other men—she hasn't seen the world. She knows nothing of life." He fixed his gaze on Molly. "I gave her a summer in France when she turned twenty-one. That's all the traveling she's ever done."

Molly looked up with surprise. "Don't you realize that a lot of people never travel out of the country?"

"They don't have the opportunity," he replied quickly.

"But you do, and since you're constantly traveling and seeing the world, you think everyone who has that chance should do the same, especially your sister."

Matt seemed thoughtful for a moment. "Not necessarily. Just because the peripatetic life-style suits me, doesn't mean it'll suit her, but she should have the chance to find out before she takes root in a small town for the rest of her life."

"Krista could just be a small-town girl."

"How will she ever know unless she has something to compare it with? I don't mean she should take off tomorrow for Bombay or Istanbul. Maybe it's as simple as going to graduate school out of state for a year. She knows nothing but Dillard and Brent. She needs to understand that she has other options. You know, they've been talking about getting married for so many years that everyone in the damned town knows about it. If they don't have a wedding, they'll probably feel as if they've failed Dillard. It's ridiculous."

"I don't think it's ridiculous at all. I think it's very special. How often these days do you find a young couple as faithful to each other as Krista and Brent? Rarely. People seem to pride themselves, not on their commitments, but on their conquests." Molly fixed Matt with a deliberate gaze.

He leaned forward. "Are you somehow alluding to people like me?"

Molly shrugged and bit into her second piece of toast.

"Well, you're right about one thing, Prescott. I've dated a lot of women, and I've learned from all of them."

"What exactly have you learned?" Even as she asked the question, Molly wondered how she'd allowed herself to get drawn into a discussion about Matthew Kincaid's love life.

"Not to get married," he answered flatly. "What about you?"

"What *about* me?" she said evasively.

"Are you married?"

"No, I'm not."

"Well, then."

"My marital status has nothing to do with my ability to put on one heck of a wedding, and that's what I plan to do in Dillard ten days from now."

Matt signaled the waitress and ordered more coffee.

"And please leave the check," Molly told her.

"No," Matt countered. "Not yet. I may want something else."

The waitress looked from one to the other, shrugged and poured the coffee. Then she disappeared without leaving the check.

"Congratulations. You've shown that you have a way with waitresses."

"I'm not ready to leave yet, and I'm the one with the car."

Again, her first impression was being proven correct, Molly realized. Despite his good looks, Matthew Kincaid was a pain in the neck.

He settled his six-foot-plus frame comfortably in the booth. "We haven't finished our talk, Prescott. Molly Prescott," he said musingly. "Sounds like a New England name."

"Vermont," she snapped, "but that has nothing to do with our discussion about Krista and Brent's wedding. It seems to me that if they want to get married there's nothing you can do about it, and if *Wedding* wants to help them there's nothing you can do about that, either."

"Don't be too sure."

"You didn't change Krista's mind, did you?"

He was noncommittal.

"Or Brent's."

There was still no response.

"So don't think you can change mine. Your high-handed tactics won't make the wedding or the magazine disappear. Neither will your threats *or* your charm."

"You are tough," Matt said with admiration. "But I think you may also be a nice person. Despite the time you've spent in New York City, I still see a lot of Vermont in you. Reasonable, kind, willing to listen in spite of yourself."

He was softening her up again. Molly steeled herself. "I left Vermont a long time ago, Mr. Kincaid."

He ignored that. "You're nice enough to realize that Krista will have a chance at a whole new kind of life if you just go away and take the wedding with you."

"Marriage *is* a new kind of life," Molly countered. "And you've overlooked one important point, Mr. Kincaid. These kids are in love."

"In love?" Matt hooted. "Come on, Prescott, give me a break. They're in love with the idea of love. And along you come with your plans for a big fancy wedding. Naturally, they're taken in. Well, go after someone else, one of the other thousands of couples who entered your contest. Go invade their lives. And once you've gone, Krista will calm down. I'll talk to her about alternatives, and the wedding will be forgotten."

Molly pushed away her plate, folded her arms on the table, and asked, "Do you know what I think? I think the problem is you."

Molly saw a flicker of anger in Matt's eye. A muscle tightened along his jaw. She realized it would be wise to ease off. But she'd gone this far, and there was no stopping her now.

"I assume you're going to fill me in on all my character flaws." He raised a dark blond eyebrow. "It's the kind of conversation I really enjoy."

"I don't know all of your flaws, Mr. Kincaid, only a few. You're a cynic. You don't believe in love or marriage. You can't understand how two people can really love each other and want to spend their lives together."

"Is that all?"

"That's all. But your cynicism isn't going to ruin this wedding. Brent and Krista have the perfect formula for a happy marriage—they know each other well and they respect each other."

"So you measure happiness by familiarity rather than intensity? That's a boring concept, Prescott."

Boring. The same word that Jeri had used. Molly frowned. "It's not boring at all. Krista and Brent aren't just some oversexed couple who met at a singles bar and decided to get married a week later."

"Let's backtrack a little, Prescott. First of all, I'm not a cynic, I'm a realist."

"Whatever you want to call it."

"Furthermore, what's the matter with sex?"

"Nothing is the matter with sex." Molly fought against the irritation she felt at this man. "The phrase was oversexed."

"You'll have to define it."

That was too much. He was still goading her, and Molly knew that she'd have to be careful not to lash out at him and get herself in real trouble. "What I think about sex isn't the topic...."

"But sex is a pretty interesting topic. There's something very exciting about making love with someone you're just getting to know. There's a sense of mystery, adventure, discovery." His eyes mocked her. "Very different from getting into bed with someone you know everything about."

He was getting to her, Molly knew that, and what was worse, he seemed to be enjoying it. "I'm not talking about getting into bed. I don't care about that."

"You don't care about getting into bed? Why, Prescott, you must really lead a boring life." His mouth quirked in the beginning of another smile.

"We're talking about the wedding," she reminded him. "It's going to happen whether you like it or not. You can't distract me."

But he had distracted her, and Molly knew it. So did Matt. She waited for his mocking smile, but it didn't come. He just looked at her silently.

"So you might as well be a good loser and get with the program," she said adamantly. "You're not going to get your way this time."

She stood up.

"Are you going somewhere?"

"I—"

Matt reached out and grabbed her arm. She tried to pull away, but he held on to her. "Sit down, Prescott. I'm not through."

His hands were very strong, and his grip was unbreakable. Molly didn't have much choice. She sat down.

Matt still hadn't let go of her arm. He held on tightly as he leaned close to speak to her. His voice was calm, but under the steadiness Molly heard a deep determination. It held her in its spell, forced her to listen.

"I'm a very bad loser, Prescott. That's because I seldom lose. I don't know how."

She raised her chin defiantly and tried to ignore the pressure of his hand on her arm. "Neither do I, Mr. Kincaid.",

"So this battle isn't over. And we're at loggerheads. There're ten days to go. A hell of a lot can happen in ten days."

"Are you planning sabotage of some kind? Because if you are . . ."

"What will you do?"

"Well, I'll . . ."

"Call the wedding police?" Matt laughed and released her arm. "Prescott, you're so dramatic. I'm not planning anything. But I might as well tell you that I'll do whatever's necessary to see that the wedding doesn't come off." He looked at her intently, their gaze locked and she saw something more than anger, and less than admiration, in his eyes. Their blue overtones had turned to a steely gray.

"Even if you break your sister's heart?"

He reached for the check and pulled some bills out of his pocket. "Hearts are easily mended, Prescott."

"How would you know?" she murmured.

Matt laughed again and stood up. "You malign me. I'm not such a bad guy. I just know what I want."

"So do I," Molly said. "I know exactly what I want— for this wedding to be not just the Wedding of the Month but the Wedding of the Year. Of the decade, in fact. If you try to stop me, you'll be very sorry."

"You talk a good game, Prescott, but you don't have a chance."

Molly swept out of the restaurant ahead of him. "For once in your lifetime, Mr. Kincaid, you've met your match. You just don't know it yet."

HALF AN HOUR LATER, Matt had navigated the turnpikes surrounding Denver and headed across the plains toward Dillard. Molly managed to fall asleep even though the stereo was playing more loudly than necessary. Any other time, she would have objected adamantly, but she'd had enough of arguing with Matt Kincaid and was determined to ignore him and his manners. Using her red cardigan as a pillow, she rested her head against the door.

Matt glanced at her quickly and then looked back again, mesmerized. Her brown hair fell in soft curls around her heart-shaped face. She seemed very young and vulnerable, nothing like the fierce woman who'd taken him on in the airport restaurant.

He'd really thought at first he might make some headway with her, convince her to give another couple the prize wedding, make her understand that if she backed off he could get Krista to postpone the wedding. In fact, he'd expected to put her back on the plane for New York.

Prescott hadn't given an inch. The more she'd dug her heels in, the stronger he'd come on, and still she hadn't backed down. Some of the things he'd said were totally out of line, but he hadn't been able to stop himself. There was something about her that made him want to push her buttons. He liked the way her eyes blazed and her cheeks flushed.

He glanced at her again out of the corner of his eye. She'd worn a turtleneck sweater under the cardigan, and it clung to the upper part of her body like a glove to a hand. The soft wool molded her firm breasts and showed the faint outline of her nipples.

Matt smiled to himself and realized he was having intense erotic thoughts about Molly Prescott after knowing her only a couple of hours. He wondered what it might be like to explore her softness under the sweater, to touch the round curve of her breasts, to feel the silkiness of her skin.

Then he laughed aloud, imagining her reaction. She'd probably cut his hand off.

Molly Prescott wasn't what he'd expected, to say the least; she was nothing like the long-legged blondes he met on ski slopes or the sassy redheads that crowded around him après-ski. But she was a very interesting woman, indeed.

And his laugh had woken her up, Matt realized.

Molly thought she'd heard laughter, but decided she must have been dreaming as she roused herself and looked around. The traffic had thinned out, and the tangled web of turnpikes had given way to one long narrow ribbon of highway that cut across the snow-packed plains. The sun was so bright that she had to shield her eyes.

"Do you have sunglasses?" Matt asked.

"Somewhere." Molly rummaged around in her purse for the glasses case. Then she pulled down the visor and glanced at herself in the mirror before putting them on. To her surprise, the face that was reflected there was pink and glowing, the eyes bright and a little defiant. She didn't look like a woman who'd traveled all night across two-thirds of a continent. She looked refreshed and ready for anything. Maybe it was the cold clear air, or maybe it was the idea of a challenge ahead. She put on the glasses and then turned to look at Matt.

"Thanks for the suggestion. There's really a glare."

"The sun reflecting on the snow and the lack of clouds will do it every time. It's called Colorado."

"Well, I must admit, it certainly is pretty."

They crested a long hill and Molly's breath caught in her throat when she got her first view of the little town at the foot of the mountains. The jagged peaks created a violent backdrop for the peacefulness of the town nestled against them. Above it all was the vast blue sky.

"So much sky," she murmured.

"I know. Everyone says that. Especially people who've lived in concrete cities where snatches of blue are only visible between buildings. Even then, it's not blue—it's more like gray or even brown, depending on the degree of smog. Here the sky is true blue, and it's everywhere."

Molly marveled again at the view and began to understand what she'd heard from Westerners and always ignored: this was big sky country, God's country.

"So much snow, too," Molly added.

"Yep, and it's likely to snow again in the next couple of days. Now, won't that be a problem for your June wedding, Prescott?"

Here we go again, Molly thought. There was no avoiding the subject. "Not at all. We've already been in touch with several companies that have snowblowing equipment. We'll get rid of the snow on the porch and in the yard surrounding it. My photographer is excellent at this kind of assignment. As long as he shoots in tight, we'll be fine."

"It still won't look like June," Matt cautioned. "Not in Dillard, Colorado in March. The sky has an entirely different quality in summertime."

"Our readers probably won't notice the quality of the sky."

"Coloradans will."

"Then I guess we'll have to avoid showing the sky as well. Or my photographer can change the *quality* simply by using a filter," Molly said smugly. "It's not going to work, Mr. Kincaid, trying to scare me off with all the problems I'll face. I know the problems. I can handle them."

Matt was quiet for a moment. Then Molly heard a low chuckle. "Even me?"

"Especially you, Mr. Kincaid. You're easily handled." Molly looked at his profile and noticed the glimmer of a smile. More than anything, she wanted to wipe that smile off his face. That would happen in time.

"I'm beginning to think this wedding is a particularly important one for you, Prescott. Could it be that you're using it to forward your own career?"

The remark—so out of the blue—stunned Molly. She lowered her eyes. In a way, what he said was true. She was counting on this wedding to be special. It appealed to her in a way no wedding had for a long time.

She thought about the fiascoes she'd dealt with in the past and gave an involuntary shudder. She'd accused Matt earlier of being a cynic, but if anything could make a person cynical, it was seeing couples marry for all the wrong reasons. Molly was sure she knew why so many of the marriages she'd covered for the magazine hadn't lasted. The couples had married within a few months of meeting. In contrast, Brent and Krista had known each other for years. They were ready for marriage and they deserved a perfect wedding. Molly had every intention of pulling it off, with their cooperation, which she didn't expect would be a problem. As for Matt, he was trouble. With a capital T. First, she'd put him in his place, then she'd find someone else to walk Krista down the aisle.

She met Matt's eyes squarely. "You're right when you say this wedding is important to me. But it's also important to Krista and Brent. And if you really love your sister, you'll butt out."

"So the battle isn't over yet?"

Molly just smiled as they approached Dillard. "It looks like a lovely town."

Matt glanced over at her. She was going to be a handful, but in a way he was looking forward to it. He hadn't had a good challenge since K 2. "It's a comfortable little town. Nothing much happens, and that's the way the folks like it here. Would you be interested in some of the history?"

"Of course." Molly pulled out her tape recorder. "Do you mind?"

"Back to business, huh?"

Again Molly didn't respond, determined not to rise to any of his verbal nudges. She turned on the pocket recorder.

"Well, I'm happy to be your tour guide. Let's see. We're on Main Street now. But we can take a detour." He turned up a side street. "Dillard was settled in the late 1800s as a mining center. The veins played out within a couple of decades, but during that time lots of people made big money and built all these Victorian houses."

They were set back from the tree-lined street on huge lots, houses with big front porches, high pointed roofs, and gingerbread facades gaily painted in pinks, blues and greens. "They're exquisite," Molly said.

"Hell to heat in winter, as those of us who came along later discovered. A few old families stayed around after the gold bust, but they had hard times until the tourists discovered Dillard. Now it's ski country in the winter and dude ranching in the summer, and everybody's pretty prosperous."

"Including Matt Kincaid."

"I get by, but not as a mountain climber. Most of my income is from the store. Kincaid Mountaineering and Sporting Goods, Limited."

"Sounds like that takes care of most outdoor endeavors."

"The more adventurous ones, anyway. If you do it in the wild, we'll outfit you." He glanced over at Molly, but she managed to avoid his mischievous look. "I guess you're a big winter sports fan, Prescott, coming from Vermont. You ski a lot?"

"I've never skied in my life. Nor have I ever climbed a mountain. I'm allergic to the outdoors."

"We'll just have to give you a taste of it while you're here."

"No thanks. Even wildflowers give me hay fever."

Matt laughed. "It's winter, Prescott. There're no wildflowers around. No flowers of any kind."

"Yes, that's going to present a problem for the wedding." Molly looked out at the snow-covered yards. Even where there were bare patches, the grass was brown. She realized that getting rid of the snow on the yards would be pointless. She didn't have a budget to bring in sod. Even without Matt Kincaid to contend with, this wedding was definitely going to be a challenge.

"You'll think of something," Matt said.

"I'm sure I will."

"Next on the agenda, downtown Dillard."

Matt obviously wished to change the subject, which was fine with Molly. "Is there such a thing? From my experience covering weddings across the country, it seems as though downtowns have disappeared and shopping malls have taken over."

"Not here. This is one of the few downtown restorations that's really worked. All of the buildings have been restored to their original turn-of-the-century architecture. It not only looks good, it's successful. The stores and restaurants are thriving, including Kincaid Mountaineering. Would you like to see it?"

"Of course." Molly was beginning to forget her jet lag. She felt up to anything.

Matt swung back to Main Street and parked. "The downtown area is closed to traffic. Do you mind a five-minute walk?"

"I'm game." Molly put away the tape recorder.

Matt was on his way around to open her door when Molly got out on her own, took a few steps to the icy sidewalk—and slipped. She tottered dangerously, flinging out her arms and fighting for balance. Matt arrived just in time to keep her upright, his hand firm under her arm.

"First thing on your shopping list is a pair of hiking boots."

"Thanks," she mumbled, trying not to let him see her embarrassment as she regained her footing. "But I told you, Mr. Kincaid, I don't go for outdoor sports."

"Here in Colorado, walking down the street is an outdoor sport. Come on, let's get you some boots."

The five-minute walk took more like twenty minutes as Matt stopped to greet friends along the way and, from what Molly could tell, everyone seemed to be his friend. Clearly, Matt was a celebrity; just as clearly, he didn't mind Molly knowing about it. It was a display of one-upmanship. This was his town; she was an interloper.

If the people on the street were friendly, the girls in Kincaid Mountaineering were downright sycophantic. Molly barely managed to keep a straight face as the sales staff—all young, all female, all beautiful—fell over themselves to please their boss.

Vying for his attention, one of them bragged about the four sets of skis she'd sold to a family of tourists. Another insisted on modeling a new lightweight parka that had just arrived. A third cooed that she didn't mind at all working Krista's shift and her own; if Matt needed her, she could even work over the weekend.

Just when Molly was beginning to find the whole scene sickening, Matt put a stop to it. "Okay, gang. There're customers in the store. Back to work. I'm going to find a pair of hiking boots for Ms. Prescott."

The staff scattered as Matt led Molly to the back of the store, sat her down and went over to the shelves. Quickly, he found what he was looking for.

"How do you know my size?"

"Years in the business. One look can tell, but just to be safe, stand up and take off your shoes."

"I really don't—"

"Come on, Prescott. Snow's predicted, and I don't want you falling on my steps and suing the hell out of me. Now take off your shoes."

Molly did as she was told, and he measured her stockinged foot, holding on to her ankle far longer than

necessary. "Just as I thought. Six and a half narrow."
He opened a box, pulled out a boot and put it on her.
It seemed enormous.

"I can't wear this thing. It must weigh a ton."

"Actually, it's very light. Lift your foot."

Molly was amazed to discover that the brown leather
boot was comfortable and, as Matt said, very light.
"It'll take years to lace up," Molly said, trying to find
something to complain about, not wishing to be in
agreement with Matt about anything if she could help
it. "And I can't wear boots with a skirt. That would
look ridiculous."

"First complaint—you lace the boots once, and after
that you only have to tighten the top. Second complaint—look around you. Everybody wears them—
with skirts, with dresses, with pants. It's de rigueur,
Prescott."

"Then why are you wearing cowboy boots?" Molly
thought she had him.

"When I dress up I wear these. Of course, I wanted
to dress up to meet the editor of *Wedding* magazine."

MOLLY BOUGHT THE BOOTS. She wore them out of the
store, feeling completely bottom heavy and off balance but managing to stand upright. Then she began
to enjoy them, walking along with assurance and a
semblance of belonging in Colorado.

She wasn't giving in to Matt's friendliness, however;
she still didn't trust him. Back in the car, he continued
the tour, turning down a curvy road and stopping by

another old Victorian house. Then he looked over at her and said with relish, "This one's ours."

"It's beautiful." The sight of it set Molly's mind going, imagining what the wide porch would look like strung with garlands of spring and summer flowers, with big pots of lilies lining the steps. She foresaw no problem in photographing the house and even the end of the brick walkway that led to it, without including the snow-filled yard. It would work! Now, if the florists in Dillard could only come up with all the flowers she needed. Even if they couldn't, Denver wasn't far away.

Eager to see more, Molly opened the car door.

This time she didn't get far. "Just a minute, Prescott." Matt reached out and grabbed her arm.

"What's the matter, Mr. Kincaid? I have boots on now. What's the problem?"

"Just that—Mr. Kincaid. Prescott. Even though you and I don't see eye to eye on this wedding—"

"That's an understatement," she interrupted.

"It doesn't mean we can't be friends."

"Mr. Kincaid, I'm here for the wedding and nothing else."

"Then for the sake of the wedding, for Krista's sake, we can try to achieve, if not friendship, at least peaceful coexistence."

Molly bit back a retort. She wouldn't come around to his way of thinking in a million years, but he was right about their relationship. There was no reason to involve Krista or Brent in it. They were a young couple on the verge of the happiest time of their lives, and both she and Matt were mature enough not to bicker in front of them.

"I want this to be a wonderful time for Krista," Molly said. "She obviously knows how you feel about the wedding so arguing in front of her solves nothing. I'm willing to bury the hatchet for Krista's sake."

"Great. For starters, you call me Matt. I'll call you Molly."

"That seems sensible," Molly agreed. "I was tired of the Mr. Kincaid bit, anyway."

"Fine. You and I can share our views about this wedding in private. I'm sure after you've been here for a while, you'll come around to my way of thinking."

"Not a chance," she said. "There's going to be a wedding."

"We'll leave that discussion for later. In the meantime, can we have a truce?"

Molly stuck out out her hand. "Absolutely. Truce."

Matt took her hand, but he didn't shake it. Instead, he pulled her close—in a movement so quick she had no time to respond—and kissed her.

The kiss took Molly so much by surprise that a brief moment passed before she tried to pull away, and then it was too late. He wouldn't let her go. One of his hands cupped the back of her head, and the other was anchored firmly at her waist. Her breasts were crushed against his chest, and her mouth was covered by his. It wasn't a gentle, feathery, friendly kiss. It was intimate and demanding.

She opened her mouth slightly to protest, and Matt took instant advantage. His tongue slid between her lips, invading her mouth. Molly continued to push against him, but he only held tighter, so tight that she could hear the thudding of his heart and the deep rasp of his breath.

Her own heart raced crazily, and a warm flush permeated her skin. How could she be so damned hot when the snow was all around them? This was getting out of hand. She had to get away.

It wasn't possible. Matt prevented it.

He seemed in no hurry to end his lengthy and thorough exploration of her mouth. She felt the warmth of his lips and sampled the taste of his mouth. A little tremor went through her. She felt enraptured, and it was a feeling that scared her to death. This couldn't happen! With all her strength, she managed to struggle out of his grasp.

"Stop it!" she shouted. "Let me go. Are you insane?"

Their faces were inches apart. Molly's eyes blazed into his. Matt's eyes glittered with laughter and his voice was mocking. "Does a man have to be insane to kiss you, Molly? Can't he do it simply for the pleasure?" He played casually with a tendril of her hair. "And it was pleasurable."

"No," she shot back, pushing his hand away.

"But now that we're friends—"

"I agreed to a truce, not fraternization with the enemy." As she finally wiggled away from him, Molly caught a glimpse of movement on the front porch. "Someone saw us!"

"It's only Krista."

"Great," Molly muttered, frantically thinking of an excuse for her behavior.

Matt swung open his door and got out. "Don't worry. Krista has lots of class. She'll never mention that she saw us necking in the driveway."

Molly thought about throwing her purse at his head. She would be able to hurt him, too, because her aim was pretty good. Not in front of Krista, she decided. Not in front of the Bride of the Month. Instead, Molly unclenched her fists, forced a smile on her lips and opened the door on her side.

"Hi, Krista," she called out with a cheery wave. "I'm Molly Prescott, and I'm here to help you put on the greatest wedding Dillard's ever seen."

4

MOLLY STRUCK OUT across the yard toward Krista, rushing to get ahead of Matt. Her cheeks still flamed from their encounter, but she kept her head high as her boots dug into the soft snow. The crunching sound encouraged her; it denoted stability. At least she wasn't going to fall down.

As Krista approached, Molly held out her hand, but Krista ignored it and enveloped her in a big hug. "You're here! I was getting worried. Was the plane late again? Was your baggage held up?"

The questions followed rapidly on each other, and Molly barely had a chance to answer, much less worry about the spark of curiosity in the young woman's eyes.

"No, the plane was on time, and I just had carry-on...."

"Then you and Matt must have been busy getting acquainted." There was the glint again. Krista had seen at least some of what went on in the front seat. As he'd speculated, she was too polite to mention it.

"Your brother gave m._ a tour of Dillard." Molly displayed a newly booted foot. "And I bought these at Kincaid Limited."

Krista's smile was wide and fabulous, revealing perfect white teeth that Molly noted with pleasure, thinking what a cover model this girl was going to make.

"Then you've met my bridesmaids."

"The girls at the shop?"

"Yes, Alison, Diane and Lisa. We all went to school together, and since I'm getting married at home, I thought I should keep my bridesmaids to three. But we never discussed that, did we? Is three too many?"

Krista, in her excitement, seemed to have a habit of bunching up her questions. It was a trait that showed her enthusiasm and endeared her to Molly.

"No to both questions," Molly said. All three girls were bubbly and pretty, just like the bride-to-be. Of course, with her blue eyes, golden hair and creamy, flawless skin, Krista was by far the prettiest, and that was as it should be. With Molly's guidance, advice and expertise, there was no doubt Krista could be the bride of the year, even of the decade.

Her arm still around Molly, Krista led her up the steps to the front porch. "Brent and I still can't believe ours will be the Wedding of the Month." She looked over Molly's shoulder. "My brother's back home to give me away. Isn't that exciting?" Quickly, she added another question. "What could be more wonderful?"

"I can't imagine." Molly didn't look back, but she knew Matt was right behind them.

"I guess you know Matt's not wild over this wedding," Krista said lightly. She shot a glance at her brother and flashed another incredible smile, seemingly unperturbed by his opinion.

"Well, I'm here to change his mind," Molly announced.

Coming up behind, Matt raised a cynical eyebrow, which Molly ignored as she changed the subject. "The porch is fantastic, Krista. Much wider than I'd expected." The floorboards and railings were painted blue to match the shutters on the two-story gray house. "There'll be room for lots of big planters of lilies and paper white narcissus—"

"Those are spring and winter flowers, aren't they?" Matt asked.

Molly hated being interrupted, especially when she wasn't talking to Matt, but to his sister. She answered grudgingly, "They're wedding flowers, no matter the season. We'll fill in with summer flowers planted around the house."

"Let's hope there's not an extreme drop in temperature," Matt said dryly.

His sister spoke up. "There won't be, Matt. Not on my wedding day." With that, she led Molly through the front door and into the high-ceilinged foyer. "It's a little old-fashioned," she apologized, gesturing to the huge hall, paneled in oak to the wainscoting and papered above in a flowered pattern.

"It's lovely," Molly said. So traditional, it was more than she'd hoped for.

"Not too Victorian? Not too corny?"

"It's perfect. An old-fashioned wedding for an old-fashioned couple."

"I guess we are old-fashioned, and if Brent were here, he'd be carrying your luggage." Krista looked around. "Where is it? Matt, where's Molly's luggage?"

Molly and Matt both answered at once.

"It's in the car—"

"I left it in the car—"

"Why?" Krista asked.

So they wouldn't drown each other out, Molly waited for Matt to answer. He didn't. Instead he stood there, tall and lanky, in the middle of the two-story-high foyer without being dwarfed.

Finally, Molly told Krista, "There's no reason to bring my bags in. Matt can help unload when I get to my hotel."

"Hotel?" Krista looked at her brother. "Didn't you tell her?"

Matt shrugged and leaned back against a marble-topped sideboard that sat just inside the hall door. "We had so much to discuss that I must have forgotten. I wasn't sure how long Pres—uh, Molly, would be staying."

"Until after the wedding," Krista said with finality.

"I think that's up to Molly—as well as where she's going to stay."

"At the hotel," Molly said. "My office made the reservation—"

"No, Molly, you're staying here," Krista said.

"I'm booked at the Dillard Inn."

"It'll be much better here. It'll be wonderful," Krista bubbled. "We can talk about the wedding from morning to night."

Molly caught a glimpse of Matt out of the corner of her eye. He looked displeased, and that was enough to convince her to stay at the Kincaid house. "Well, if you're really sure, Krista—"

"Absolutely."

Matt headed out to retrieve Molly's luggage, and both women looked after him with their own special smiles.

"Now, tell me what you think about the house," Krista urged.

It was just what Molly had hoped for and more. Especially the staircase—broad, wide and curving. The second floor was wrapped by a balcony and gave a feeling of openness and light.

"Wow is what I think," Molly said warmly. "I can just see you coming down the stairway in your wedding gown, the long train flowing behind you."

"About the dress, I never had any response from the descriptions I sent you."

"That's because I had to meet you before I decided— see the house and feel the ambience."

"I chose my favorites from the ones that were available here."

"Very pretty they were, too, but we might find something even better back in New York."

"In New York? Could I get a dress from New York in time?"

"Of course," Molly told her.

Just then they heard Matt at the doorway, dropping her bags onto the floor. "And now that you've felt the ambience..." Molly watched as he flung his Stetson toward a brass antique coatrack, hit the mark perfectly, then rake his fingers through his tousled hair. "What do you think?" He shrugged out of his jacket and hung it beside the hat.

She expected he was waiting for her to say something foolish to give him an opening for one of his sarcastic remarks.

"I think it's a beautiful Victorian setting that calls for a beautiful Victorian dress."

"And Molly can order it from New York in time for the wedding," Krista added.

"I've brought catalogs from some of the major New York designers. We'll go through them tonight and pick out a spectacular dress." She spoke conspiratorially to Krista, ignoring her brother completely. "It'll be airfreighted within two days, and we can have the alterations done here if necessary. I'd guess that you're about five foot seven. . . ."

"Seven and a half," Krista corrected. "And I'm a size eight."

"What could be more perfect! Do I know how to pick a bride or what? Not only gorgeous with a glorious house, but a perfect size eight. This is—"

"'Scuse me, ladies," Matt broke in. "I hate to interrupt this love feast, but where do you want Molly's bags?"

"In the guest room, of course," Krista said airily. "I'm not sure I'm a perfect size eight," she told Molly.

"Do you ever need to have clothes altered?"

"Well, no . . . ."

"Then you're perfect."

They both laughed as Matt picked up the bags and headed for the stairway. "I'll just get lunch ready," Krista informed her. "Soup and banana bread. Is that okay? Will it be enough?"

Molly answered both questions with a yes, and followed Matt up the stairs.

"I'll see you in the kitchen in a few minutes," Krista called over her shoulder.

"I'll be right down."

"Yours is the first room on the right." Matt climbed the stairs ahead of Molly. "Mine's the first on the left."

"We won't be using your room in the story, so there's no need for me to see it," Molly shot back.

Could there have been any way for her to ignore the rear view of Matt as he climbed the stairs? Molly figured she could have waited for him to get to the top and then followed. Or looked the other way as she climbed. Or closed her eyes. Those were the choices, and she opted for none of them. Instead, she took advantage of her first close look at Matt Kincaid from behind.

Face it, Molly, she told herself, *you like what you see.* Well-muscled back in a snug wool plaid shirt; slim waist; long muscular legs that tested the denim fabric of his jeans. And anchoring everything perfectly, a firm bottom that curved just enough to tempt Molly's eyes—and make her blush.

He was physically compelling...and very irritating. Maybe she'd pass both those observations on to Jeri when she called New York later. Molly was still angry about their kiss, but she certainly wouldn't mention it to Jeri. Or to Matt. Oh, no. She'd ignore it and show him that it meant nothing to her. She'd make it clear that his ploy to make her feel uncomfortable and put her on the defensive hadn't worked.

Matt pushed open the door to the guest room and stepped aside for Molly to enter. She was instantly charmed. The eggshell white walls contrasted with the fine, dark sheen of the woodwork. White lace curtains hung at the windows, which were flanked by a walnut chest of drawers and a rocking chair. There was a feeling of spareness and space, combined with a welcoming comfort.

"What a great room," she murmured. "I love the bed."

She fell onto the flowered comforter that covered the brass bed.

Matt placed her bags on the luggage rack. "It belonged to my parents, handed down from my grandmother. Krista bought a new mattress not long ago, but I haven't had a chance to try it out yet." He paused, leaning against the door jamb with one hip jutting forward and his arms folded across over his chest. It was a macho stance that Molly found particularly annoying. Grinning broadly, he waited.

"I'll let you know how it is."

"I'd appreciate that."

He made no move to leave. Molly busied herself by unzipping a bag and haphazardly pulling things out.

He still didn't leave, and she couldn't ignore him indefinitely. "Thanks for bringing up my bags." She used a dismissive tone.

"You're welcome."

"Do you want something else?"

"I want lots of things." He leisurely swept his eyes up and down her body.

Molly felt as if she were too close to an open fire; her body tingled and grew warm as his lazy eyes inspected her. Were they blue or gray? She couldn't decide, and that infuriated her even more. When Molly finally responded, she attempted to make her voice as icy as the snow outside.

"I didn't ask to stay here. Your sister invited me. I've accepted because it's something she wants. So if you and I must be under the same roof, let's try not to get on each other's nerves."

"What do you mean? You're not getting on my nerves at all."

"Well, you're getting on mine. With remarks like . . . well . . . snide sexual innuendos."

Matt's face broke into another wide grin. "Prescott, you're amazing. You manage to bring up the subject of sex at every opportunity. Now, I'm not sure what you mean by 'snide sexual innuendos.' What I actually had in mind was your backing down about the wedding, the ceremony being called off and Krista's going to graduate school. Those were the things I wanted to talk about. Nothing sexual at all." He shook his head slowly. "You really do have an active imagination."

Cheeks burning, Molly decided to get out of the conversation while she had a chance. "Excuse me, Mr. Kincaid, but I'd like to freshen up before lunch, so—"

"The bath's right through that door. I'm sure you'll find it appropriately Victorian, just right for your magazine. See you at lunch, Prescott, and try not to talk about sex in front of my little sister. You sophisticated New York types can be a bad influence on us out here in the heartland."

"Weren't we going to use first names, *Matt?*" she asked.

"Of course, *Molly*. Thanks for reminding me."

He'd managed to get the last word, Matt realized as he sauntered down the steps, hands in his pockets, still grinning but not altogether amused. Molly Prescott could be a pain, but she was also a damned intriguing woman. He'd only been back in Dillard a week, and he was getting bored already. He had no interest in Krista's friends, the adoring sales staff at the store. As for the other women in Dillard, he'd dated most of them from time to time, and they didn't dazzle him, either. On the other hand, Molly excited him enormously.

He hadn't intended that to happen. He'd expected her to be back on a plane heading for New York by now, but she wasn't. She was settling into the guest room of his family home in Dillard. That was already too much; but there was more. She was just down the hallway from him. Convenient.

Matt chuckled softly. Every time he got near her he could feel the electricity between them. She felt it, too; of that he was certain. He remembered their kiss. Her lips had been like velvet, warm and soft and sensual. Molly was a real challenge, and Matt lived for challenges. She was unknown territory waiting to be explored. He had no idea what would happen the next time they were alone together, but he knew it wouldn't be boring. Nothing about Molly would ever be boring.

MOLLY CHANGED into jeans and a fresh turtleneck sweater, combed her hair and pinned it back in a seashell whorl. She was calm, cool and collected. At least, that was her resolve, and she entered the kitchen, a woman in charge. No matter what Matt Kincaid did or said, she couldn't be compromised.

The three of them settled at the table. Just as Krista served up the soup, there was a knock at the back door.

"That's Brent," Krista guessed.

"The other half of our perfect couple—I can't wait to meet him," Molly responded. She expected a rebuttal from Matt, but he was silent, his face guileless, as he cut into the loaf of banana bread.

Brent brought with him a swoosh of fresh, chilled air from outdoors and another freshness that was all his own. He dropped a light kiss on Krista's cheek and then enthusiastically shook hands with Molly. "Am I pleased to meet you, Ms. Prescott. We can't believe that we've been chosen for the lead story in *Wedding* magazine."

Molly greeted him effusively. "You were the natural choice, Brent. And you're to call me Molly." Quickly, Molly judged Brent photogenically on a scale of one to ten and arrived at a nine and a half. Just under six feet of lean and lanky pleasantness, topped with brown hair and eyes. His coloring contrasted wonderfully with Krista's blond good looks. Molly could easily visualize them on the cover of *Wedding*. "You and Krista are just what the magazine needs. A breath of fresh air."

"Cold mountain air," Brent joked as he slipped into a chair and accepted the bowl of soup Krista offered. "I'm not sure how you're going to pull off a June wedding in Colorado in March when we're still anticipating another blizzard or two before the end of the season."

"Nothing to it," Molly replied. "I've done Christmas weddings in August and fall weddings in May."

"Molly's a together person," Matt commented.

Molly smiled tightly. Then, calm and in charge of herself, she dictated, "We need to get down to the details. Planning a wedding is like launching a rocket. It's countdown time."

"Countdown. Rocket launching. Those are interesting images," Matt observed.

Molly suddenly realized that she'd left her metaphors open to an interpretation that could be sexual, especially if Matt was doing the interpreting.

"You New York editors are so . . . imaginative," he added.

Molly realized that the best defense was to avoid the attack, change the subject, and move on. "Now, about the wedding, have you rented a tux, Matt?"

He just smiled enigmatically and asked for another bowl of soup.

"Brent?" Molly prodded.

"Well, not yet," he admitted. "I wasn't exactly sure what to get."

"It's easy," Molly said. "The wedding is daytime, noon, and formal. Cutaways for the men . . ."

"Really?" Brent asked.

"Yes. But not black."

"No?"

"No."

"What other color is there?" Brent asked.

"Gray."

"I see."

Molly laughed. "You don't really see, do you?"

"No," Brent conceded.

"Well, it's traditional for a noon wedding. Gray striped morning suit—"

"But it won't be morning," Brent interceded.

"That's just a name for the formal wear. It doesn't mean you only wear it in the morning."

"I see," Brent said with a wide grin. "We may have to go to Denver."

"Then go to Denver. Today. If they're not available I need to know at once so I can have them shipped from New York. So there's the groom, best man, two groomsmen and of course the one who gives away the bride."

Matt was silent.

"Matt . . ." Krista began.

"You'll have to go with them to Denver," Molly told him.

Matt shook his head. "I'm going to the store."

"Matt . . ." Krista tried again.

"Then if you'll be good enough to leave your measurements with Brent."

"I don't have the slightest idea what my measurements are."

Molly lifted her chin defiantly and looked him straight in the eye. "Maybe you should look through your clothes and find out."

"Sorry. I just don't have the time."

"Then I suppose we'll have to go through your clothes and find them for ourselves."

"Matt . . ." Krista attempted for the third time.

"It's all right, Krista. If that's what it takes, that's what we'll do," Molly said.

Matt began to laugh. "You're too much, Prescott. I really could have used you to rally the porters on my last K2 climb. You'd have gotten us up the mountain, blizzard be damned."

"So you'll cooperate and go with the others to Denver?"

"Nope."

Molly gave up and looked over at Krista. "You've been trying to reason with him, Krista. Now it's time to give him a piece of your mind."

Matt laughed again, and Krista blushed profusely. "He's just a big tease, Molly."

"What do you mean?"

"He has all that stuff—tux, morning suit, everything."

"Gray-striped pants?" Molly asked Matt.

"Yes," Krista answered.

"Cutaway?"

"Yes. He has formal clothes for every occasion. Matt travels in very fancy circles."

Molly realized she'd overlooked that obvious fact. She'd been made a fool of by the cosmopolitan, jet-setting Matt Kincaid. She took a deep breath. "Of course. I should have known. I'll expect your morning suit to blend perfectly with the others," she threatened.

"Not a problem, Prescott. So you won't need to send out the wedding police." He winked at Molly and finished off his soup. "Krista, I'll be late tonight. I'm meeting with the accountant at the store around six." He cut another piece of banana bread to take with him. "Good luck in Denver, Brent."

With that he was out the back door before Molly had a chance to get in a last word.

"What's all that 'Prescott' business?" Krista asked as the back door closed behind her brother.

"Just Matt's idea of fun," Molly said dismissively. "Now that he's gone, let's get organized."

Brent stifled a yawn that drew a nudge from Krista.

"Don't worry, Krista, I don't expect Brent to be enthralled by all of this, but he needs to hear it. Why don't you dish up some more soup for him?"

"Good idea," Brent agreed. "My wife-to-be is a superb cook of soup and banana bread. I'm not so sure about some of her other recipes, though."

Krista ladled more soup into his bowl. "I have lots of great recipes Matt's brought back from all around the world. Very exotic dishes that he's taught me to cook."

"It's just that I'm not into exotic food," Brent explained.

"He'll learn," Krista told Molly.

While they went over the wedding plans, Molly kept assuming that Krista and Brent would be *Wedding's* most romantic couple ever, although they seemed more comfortable than romantic. As they talked to her about each other, their conversation was free and easy, like old friends who were very content in their relationship. That's just what Molly had wanted to see, love and friendship, feelings that were deep down, not just on the surface.

It was particularly refreshing that they didn't have to play games or pretend. Especially Brent, who finally stood up halfway into their discussion, stretched, and admitted defeat.

"I know just about everything I need to know. The baker has us on his calendar, but he wants the final order a few days ahead of time. Molly'll handle the florists because she wants the place filled inside and out and that could mean going to Denver for more potted flowers. Krista has two bids from caterers, and Molly expects they'll donate their services for a mention in the magazine, but if they don't *Wedding* will pick up the bill. I need to round up my groomsmen and take them in to Denver for their cutaways—gray-striped. Plus, there'll be seventy-five at the ceremony, and my mom's not too thrilled about that."

"Stop. Time out," Molly called. "That's the first I've heard about your mom."

"I thought I'd leave that one for Krista to explain," Brent admitted. "Meanwhile, you ladies have a lot of planning to do."

"In which you're involved," Molly reminded him.

"I know you'll make the right choices," he said with a grin.

"Brent—"

"Don't worry, Molly. I'll get the guys to Denver today, I promise, and we'll all come back gray-striped and perfect. Then I'll take you to dinner. About seven?"

With a quick kiss on the top of Krista's head, he was out the door.

Molly didn't stop to worry about the brevity of his kisses or the overall lack of affection between Krista and Brent. Something else was bothering her.

"What's all this about Brent's mother?"

"Oh, it's not a problem, really. She would have liked a bigger wedding—if there was going to be a wedding at all."

"What? I thought you and Mrs. Oliver were good friends. Brent's questionnaire went into that in detail."

"Of course we're friends. She just doesn't want me to marry her son."

"I don't understand."

"Oh, it's not a problem."

"Krista, you keep saying that, but it is a problem. Or it could be."

"Not really. Brent's mom just thinks I'm wrong for her son, but she's thought that for years even though she likes me very much."

"Then why?"

"I guess it has to do with Matt."

Molly heaved a sigh. "I'm not surprised."

As Krista cleared the table, she explained to Molly, "You see, my parents and Brent's parents were Coloradans...."

"Of course."

"Real Coloradans. They were born here and went to school here, just like their parents. They loved Dillard, the mountains, nature. I guess they were sort of hippies in the sixties. Matt rebelled at that."

"He certainly loves the outdoors."

"Oh, yes. He trained to climb right here in these hills but, unlike our parents, he never stayed in Dillard for very long at a time. Later on, he pushed for me to get away."

"Not successfully."

"I guess Brent's mom thinks it's just a matter of time. Brent's a small-town boy, and all he wants is to settle down here."

"Isn't that what you want?"

"Sure, but she has this crazy idea that if I get tempted with a more exciting life-style, I'll be off and going. Just because of what happened that summer in Paris."

"Oh, oh."

"It wasn't a problem, really."

"Krista, don't keep saying that and then keep following up with problems."

Krista laughed. "Let me explain. Matt sent me to France after I graduated, and I missed Brent like crazy. I really couldn't wait to get back, but—"

"But what?"

"I learned French really easily, and I adapted to the life-style, I guess. I took a couple of classes, cooking and painting. I did real well in both of them, but Brent's not crazy about French cooking, and he thought my pictures were weird. Like I said, Molly. It wasn't a problem. I don't paint anymore, and I save my cooking sprees for Matt. It's just that Suzanne thinks one day I'll suddenly start speaking nothing but French and run around in an artist's smock, munching on pâté."

Molly laughed aloud. "But you're happy here in Dillard."

"Of course I am, and I can't wait to get married. Can we look at the bridal gowns now?"

Molly relaxed. She could handle Brent's mother. "I'll get the designer book. There's also one with bridesmaids' dresses. We'll find something that coordinates with yours and order them, too."

"My bridesmaids won't get to pick out their own dresses?"

"Can you imagine three women trying to decide on one style? No, that's the responsibility of *Wedding* magazine, and since we're picking up the tab—" Suddenly Molly remembered Matt's jibe about her steamroller tactics and softened her approach. "We can take the book to the store when we narrow down the choice, and the bridesmaids can look over them with us."

"No, I guess that's not necessary," Krista conceded. "You're the one with experience, Molly. You've seen my bridesmaids. They'll look great in anything you choose."

Molly smiled in satisfaction. Things were going just the way she wanted.

AT MIDNIGHT, Molly had silently retracted that thought a dozen times as she continued to toss and turn in the big brass bed. The mattress was comfortable, the down quilt was warm and soft, and just enough moonlight trickled in to bathe the guest room in a pleasant glow.

Still, she couldn't sleep, and she couldn't dismiss the nagging worries.

She should have been relaxed and pleased over the progress they'd made during the evening. She and Krista had agreed on the wedding and bridesmaid dresses, Victorian in design, just as Molly had visualized. Brent had reported on a successful foray with his groomsmen for their cutaways. Krista had a seamstress ready and waiting in case any of the clothes needed alterations. Molly was right on schedule.

Then what was bothering her?

It must be Suzanne Oliver, Molly decided. She'd hoped for cooperation from that quarter, but she'd handled hundreds of difficult mothers of the groom and bride in the past. She could handle this one. She'd been careful not to mention any worries about Suzanne during dinner, and when Brent had brought up her views it had been with acceptance rather than concern. Molly had adopted that attitude and tried to relax. After dinner Brent had driven them back to the house and gone off to watch the basketball play-offs with his buddies. Everything was fine.

Then why couldn't Molly sleep? Finally, she decided that it must be worry about the magazine spread. Everything was so casual, so easy and friendly that Pete's photographs could end up looking boring. That was it, she wanted to capture the excitement, not just the happiness, that existed between Krista and Brent. She laughed aloud. They were so content in their lives that she was worried! Well, she and Pete could handle that easily. The spark was there; it just needed to be drawn out for the camera. She'd explain that to Krista and Brent, drop a few subtle hints to them when Pete arrived. She wasn't always a steamroller; she could apply subtlety when needed. Matt Kincaid didn't know everything about her.

Just then she heard his footsteps on the stairs, a slow measured tread. Instinctively Molly held her breath, listening. Matt seemed to hesitate at the top of the stairs. What was he waiting for? she wondered. She could feel her heart racing absurdly, which irritated her beyond measure. Yet no amount of willpower could halt the erratic pounding.

She heard his footsteps recede from her doorway. There was the sound of his door opening and closing. And then quiet. Molly pulled the covers over her head and tried not to think about Matt Kincaid sleeping just across the hall from her. It was a long time before the rapid beat of her heart gave way to a calmer, steadier rhythm. Then sleep finally came.

5

MOLLY OPENED HER EYES and looked at the clock on the bedside table. Seven a.m. She closed her eyes again. It was too early, but the slivers of bright daylight filtering through the room challenged her to get up. Besides, even after a late night, she felt wide awake. Then she remembered. It was nine o'clock in New York, and she'd be at her breakfast table, reading the *Times* and preparing for the day ahead.

She listened intently. The house was quiet. Earlier, just as she'd begun to come to consciousness, she'd heard a noise in the hallway, but now there was only silence. Never mind. She was hungry and wondered about the propriety of going downstairs to the kitchen and fixing herself some tea and toast. The more she thought about the idea, the more she liked it. Krista wouldn't mind. Hadn't she told Molly to make herself at home?

Molly tugged at her knee socks, pulled on her flannel robe and listened at the door. Nothing. Slowly she made her way down the stairs to the kitchen, feeling like an intruder, until she saw Krista's note on the counter.

You're on New York time so don't wait for me to get up. Help yourself to bread, coffee, tea, cereal, eggs, bacon and anything else you can find. Try Suzanne's homemade jam. It's great!

Happily Molly busied herself fixing tea and toast, which she spread thickly with the raspberry jam. Carrying her breakfast to the table, she thought how nice it was to have the early morning alone. She could get her bearings, then mentally go over the long list of wedding preparations.

She'd just bitten into the toast—deciding the jam was good if a little too sweet—and lifted the teacup to her lips when the back door swung open and Matt Kincaid burst into the room like an avalanche.

"Prescott, you're up. I'm surprised. I never would have taken you for an early riser."

He was wearing a navy blue sweat suit and running shoes. When he made his way to the refrigerator and pulled out a jug of orange juice, she noticed his shirt bore a Kincaid Mountaineering logo along with a slogan: Do it in the Wild.

"It's nine-thirty in New York," she informed him. Suddenly she became aware of the intimate setting. Here she was, the senior editor of a national magazine, sitting in Matt Kincaid's kitchen in her flannel robe and knee socks, which did not exactly convey the sophisticated image she'd hoped to maintain. Matt's respect, if not his admiration, was important if Molly was going to pull off the wedding without any snags. It was time to get to her room and into more appropriate clothes. It was time to get out of the kitchen and away from Matt.

While she was contemplating that action, he finished his juice, poured another glass and grabbed a towel from a pile on top of the washing machine. Wiping the perspiration from his face, he dropped down in the chair across from her and leaned forward companionably.

She'd watched each of his actions as though mesmerized, when she should have gotten up and headed for her room. Now it was too late to leave without seeming intimidated.

"If I'd known you were awake I'd have asked you to go running with me," Matt began.

"Thanks, but I'm really not a runner."

"Not a skier, not a runner. What do you do for exercise, Prescott?"

"Walk from my apartment to the office and back— a total of forty blocks."

He looked unimpressed. "I run five or six times that distance every day."

"No matter how cold?"

"Thirty-two degrees? That's not cold, Prescott. Cold is being on K2—"

"What's K2? Is that short for Kilimanjaro?" Molly asked, searching her mind for scattered information about mountain climbing. Matt burst into laughter.

"Kilimanjaro's in Africa."

"I knew that," she defended. "Ernest Hemingway and the *Snows* . . ."

"K2's in Pakistan, and she's—well, she's no lady. As tall as Everest but meaner and tougher. A real man-killer."

Molly didn't miss the gender references but withheld comment on them.

"When you're at twenty-two thousand feet, and it's thirty below zero with the wind blowing eighty miles an hour..."

"Why in the world would you subject yourself to those conditions?"

"Because it's there?"

"You can do better than that, Kincaid." She wasn't unaware that they'd gone back to using last names.

"You ask why, I ask why not. Why not climb the meanest she-devil of a mountain in the world? Why not experience the excitement and adventure of a lifetime all rolled into a couple of months? You like excitement, don't you?"

"Excitement is one thing, courting danger is another."

"The two often go together, or haven't you learned that yet?"

"I live in New York," she said icily. "I know all about danger from just traveling on the subway." She pushed back her chair. It was time to get out of there, but she needed an excuse. "I'm going to make another cup of tea and take it up to my room. Would you like one?"

"Nope, I'm not much of a tea drinker. I'll have breakfast later with Krista." He smiled at Molly with the measuring grin that she'd come to know and dread, but his next remark was unexpected. "You look great in the morning, Prescott. Very young and vulnerable. Pink's a good color on you. In fact that whole outfit—"

Molly held her breath, waiting for the insult.

"—makes you look about twelve years old. I bet you're wearing fuzzy slippers, too."

She tried to hide her feet beneath the table.

"Pink, I'll bet." His eyes were dancing, and Molly knew he was loving every minute of his teasing.

She stuck out her foot.

"I don't believe it—socks!"

"And blue socks at that, not pink. That shows what you know about women."

He sipped his juice and looked at her speculatively. "What I know about women isn't the point, Prescott. It's that I know you wear a pink flannel robe, blue socks, and lack excitement in your life."

Molly headed for the stove, aware that if she hadn't announced her intentions of having a second cup, she'd be on her way now, out of the kitchen and out of Matt's range.

He was waiting for a response.

"I'm not here for excitement. I'm here to put on a wedding."

"But if you were here for excitement, how would last night have rated on the scale?"

The kettle whistled.

"That good, huh?"

Molly tried not to laugh. "Actually, we had a lovely dinner and afterward Krista and I chose the wedding dresses, which I'll order today."

"And what about the devoted fiancé?"

"Well, he went off to watch television—"

Matt slapped his knee. "Whatta you think about that? A real surprise, huh?"

Without responding, Molly poured the steaming water in her cup and dunked the tea bag.

"Don't you get it, Prescott? He's so much in love with my sister that he goes off to watch a ball game."

"He knew Krista and I had wedding plans to go over—"

"And he was being polite?"

"Yes."

"Then why weren't *you* polite? Why didn't you tip-toe up to bed and leave the lovebirds to themselves?"

"Because—"

"Because you know they're bored with each other. Left alone, Krista would have continued poring over the wedding catalogs, and Brent would have watched the ball game."

"Maybe so." Molly sipped her tea and tried to think of a way to justify the lovebirds' unloving behavior. "They're very comfortable with each other."

"Comfortable? They put each other to sleep, and you know it, Prescott. The last thing in the world they should do is get married. It would lead to institution-alized boredom. Krista needs to find a guy who'll break down the door to be with her."

Molly headed toward the hallway. "I don't want to hear that nonsense."

Matt was up in a shot and beat her to the door. "You need to hear it, Prescott." He blocked her exit effort-lessly with his arm. "It's a subject you've been avoid-ing."

Molly stood, looking up at Matt. He seemed awesome, barring her way. The towel still hung around his neck, and she could see the muscles in his chest and across his shoulders, even through the heavy fabric of his sweatshirt.

"I'm talking about chemistry. Excitement. Possibly even the illusion of danger. That certain something that happens between a man and a woman . . ." Absently, he'd taken a strand of her hair and was twisting it in his fingers.

Molly couldn't seem to get her breath. Was he talking about her—them? No, he must be talking about Krista and Brent. She needed to listen, to pay attention, to snap back with her usual sharp retort, but all she could do was stand there looking into his eyes.

Were they blue or gray? She still couldn't be sure. In the morning light they were constantly changing, and the flecks of gold in his irises just confused her more. She looked away from his eyes and tried to focus on something else. She noticed a scar on his cheek. Was it from childhood, she wondered, or from a climbing accident . . . ?

He was talking, and Molly struggled to listen and respond. Her mouth felt as if it were stuffed with cotton. He was so close that the heat from his body warmed her. She almost basked in it.

"And so I'd appreciate it if you'd have a talk with Krista," Molly heard him saying. "Feel her out. Tell her what you've observed between her and Brent. If she hears it from another woman's perspective, she'll realize that it can't possibly work out."

Molly finally got her breath. "There's just one problem, Matt. It *is* going to work out. They're not bored—they're happy. Their excitement comes from building a life together, not roaming around the world looking for cheap thrills. You can't understand that. You can't understand how they could be beginning a life—with no help from you."

"Wait a minute. Back up. My thrills aren't cheap, Prescott." He gave her an insinuating grin.

Molly ignored it and tried to push past him, but Matt's arm was as immovable as one of the mountains he climbed. She gave up, turned away and then remembered the cup of tea she was holding. She looked up at him, down at the steaming tea, and then back up at him.

"You wouldn't—"

"Wouldn't I?"

Matt moved away from the door. "I'm not about to find out."

Without a word, Molly swept by him and down the hallway, hoping to create a majestic image, despite the knee socks and frayed robe.

"Remember, Prescott," he called after her, "always thrills, but never cheap."

She started up the stairs as Krista came down.

"Hi, Molly, ready for breakfast?"

Molly smiled politely but didn't break stride. "No, thanks, Krista. You go ahead without me." She made it to her room and managed to refrain from slamming the door.

Matt had moved into the hallway to watch the scene unfold. When Krista reached the bottom of the stairs, he was waiting for her.

"What's going on between you two?"

"Not much."

"I saw what happened in the car yesterday."

"Anything you saw was a reflection of light on the windshield," he replied.

"Sure, Matt."

He took the stairs two at a time, whistling softly.

"Leave her alone, Matt," Krista called after him. "If you do anything to mess up this wedding, I'll—"

Matt turned and leaned over the railing. "How could I interfere with perfection, sis? You and Brent have been chosen by *Wedding* magazine to be the perfect couple. What Molly Prescott has decreed, let no man put asunder."

Matt went into his room and stripped off his sweats. His logic would prevail, and Molly knew it. Deep down she knew he was right about the wedding plans. She couldn't deny the truth of what he said; he could tell it was getting to her. It wouldn't be long before she realized how impossible the idea of marriage between Krista and Brent really was.

All he needed was a little time.

"YOU REALLY DON'T MIND if I go in to work for a while?" Krista asked Molly after lunch.

"Of course not, Krista. I realize you have other responsibilities."

"Well, I really wouldn't have to go in except we're in the middle of inventory, and Alison's out sick. I just hate to leave you on your own."

"I can certainly take care of myself, especially the way you have the guest room set up—with a desk and telephone. It's like my own office. I'll get right to work. We're ahead of schedule now that the dresses are ordered."

"And the caterer's bids are in, even though you weren't all that pleased with our choices."

"They were fine," Molly equivocated.

"Unfortunately, they're all Dillard has to offer."

"I think we can work with them to improve the menus. Quiche and pasta have been done to death. We need something that looks a little more interesting."

"What about taste?"

"If they're in the catering business, we have to assume they know how to cook, although they may not necessarily be experts at presenting the food, Krista. When we photograph the tables there should be a look of elegance and opulence to go along with the Victorian setting. So when you get right down to it, the look is probably as important as the taste. I'll see what Pete has to say."

Krista pulled on her parka. "Who's Pete?"

"Pete Walenski, our photographer. One of the best. I'm sure Dillard has never had a wedding as beautifully photographed as this one will be."

"That's exciting," Krista said. "When will he get here? Will he want to stay with us? There's an extra room—"

"I'm not sure exactly when he's arriving. I'll find out as soon as I call New York. And no, he definitely will not stay here. Definitely." Molly thought of the effect Pete had on some women, most women, in fact. "I'll book him into a hotel."

"Whatever you say." Krista was at the door. "Just remember that he's always welcome. Bye, Molly."

Halfway out the door, she seemed to have an afterthought and stepped back inside. "Suzanne Oliver may drop over today. She wants to meet you as soon as possible."

"I was afraid of that."

"Oh, don't worry. She's really a lot of fun although you might find her kind of strange. See you later."

Molly headed upstairs to call the magazine. She'd been casual about Pete to Krista, but she was becoming a little anxious. She hadn't heard a word and wondered where the hell her photographer could be.

Jeri picked up on the first ring. "I knew you'd be calling. The answer is yes. I talked to the manufacturers right after you called this morning, and the dresses will be airfreighted out first thing tomorrow."

"I knew I could count on you," Molly said warmly. "But I'm not calling about the dresses. Where's Pete? I expected him to have checked in with me by now."

"Oh, that."

"Yes, Jeri. *That*. Let's have it. What's our boy up to?"

"Well, I've been in touch with him."

"And?"

"He was riding his motorcycle out to Colorado—"

"His motorcycle! In the snow?"

"He said he was taking the southern route through Texas or something. But that's all changed anyway since the accident."

Molly forced herself not to react. It wouldn't do any good to shout or curse or berate Jeri, since it wasn't her fault. Instead she asked, "He's not hurt?"

"Pete's fine, but his Harley's a mess. So he's picking up a flight out of Houston in the next couple of days when he recovers."

"Didn't you say he was fine?"

"I guess Pete thought he deserved a little rest."

"Where was he planning to take this respite?"

"Well . . ."

"You don't know where he is, do you, Jeri?"

"Not exactly."

"Find him."

"Molly, he's not contracted to get there until a week before the wedding. There's still plenty of time, so don't worry. He'll turn up."

"Of course he will, but meanwhile I'm a nervous wreck. I don't like having all these loose ends."

"This business is full of loose ends. In fact, life is full of them."

"No time for philosophizing, Jeri. Loose ends are for tying up."

"You sound stressed out. Is everything all right?"

"It's not so bad. Krista is a dream and so is Brent. The house is perfect. Wait 'til you see the photos—when Pete gets here, *if*—"

Jeri changed the subject. "What about the brother? You haven't mentioned the hunk."

"There's no need to."

"Giving you trouble, huh?"

Molly wasn't about to go into it. "I can handle Matt Kincaid."

"Hmm. That sounds interesting. I like hearing about men who need to be handled. Tell me more."

"It's not all that interesting. He's just one more loose end to be tied up."

"Molly, don't avoid the real subject. Is he as handsome as—"

The doorbell rang, and Molly sighed with relief. "Got to go. Someone's here, and I think that someone's the mother of the groom. I'll check in later, and please find Pete, Jeri. Find him and get him moving." With a quick goodbye, Molly hung up and headed downstairs to answer the bell.

It wasn't Suzanne after all, she decided when she opened the door. The woman who stood before her didn't look anywhere near old enough to be Brent's mother. She was carrying a huge basket of what looked like weeds and wore a long suede coat draped with a brightly colored scarf. Her dark hair was pulled back and her ears were adorned with dangly silver earrings.

"Hi, you must be Molly. I'm Suzanne Oliver."

Molly was speechless as she stepped aside and let her in.

Suzanne headed for the kitchen with her box of weeds, asking over her shoulder, "Is Krista here?"

"Nope, she's at work."

"Good," Suzanne decreed. "Then we'll have some time alone to talk."

"Would you like me to make you some tea...?" Suzanne obviously had something on her mind so Molly decided cordiality was the best tactic to pursue.

"That sounds lovely, but Matt and Krista are coffee drinkers."

"I found some tea—"

"Never mind." Suzanne rummaged in the basket and came up with a small tin container. "Herbal. I make it myself." She put the basket on the window ledge. "The rest of these herbs will do nicely here where there's just enough sunlight."

"They're herbs?"

"Of course. I try to bring some over from time to time. Shall I make tea for both of us?"

"Yes, thank you."

She shed her coat, draped it over the back of a kitchen chair, and went about preparing the tea. Her earrings, bracelets and necklaces jingled as she worked. "Krista doesn't use enough natural ingredients when she cooks," she said. "Few people do these days. I grew the herbs in my greenhouse, but spring's just around the corner, and soon everything can be moved outside."

Molly had become a passive participant in the conversation and there was nothing she could do about it.

Finally, as they sat down to tea, Molly managed to turn the talk to the upcoming wedding. She'd been warned that Suzanne didn't approve, and she knew why, but she had no intention of divulging her information. Besides, Suzanne's reasoning was absurd. "I imagine you're pleased that Krista and Brent are having an at-home wedding."

"I certainly am, but unfortunately this house isn't big enough for everyone we need to invite. It really should be held outside."

"Not quite the weather for that." Molly sipped the tea, which was delicious.

"That's why they should wait until June. By which time, I imagine, they will have changed their minds."

Molly tensed. She'd known it was coming, but that statement was pretty definite.

"What makes you think that, since they haven't changed their minds in all these years?"

"Because they're both beginning to have second thoughts and by June . . ."

"You've been talking to Matt," Molly guessed.

"No, I came to that conclusion on my own when Matt was off climbing mountains on the other side of the world. Of course, there're plenty of mountains here," she added, "but he chooses to go searching them out in odd places. I never could understand that urge to travel when Dillard has everything a person could ask for."

Molly prepared herself for the onslaught.

"Brent is a hometown boy. He takes after me, not his father."

"Brent's father . . ." Molly had wondered about him.

"We married young, just like Brent and Krista are planning to do, but he was never content with the kind of life we led. When the sixties era ended and we all began to get older, he realized he wanted something more. I can't blame him. Some people are like that. They have a kind of wanderlust. Brent doesn't have it, and he never will. Matt's always had it, and so has Krista. She just doesn't realize it yet. Believe me, Molly. I've lived through it, and I know."

"Could it be that you're just afraid the same thing will happen to Brent that happened to you? Could you be personalizing a little?"

Suzanne took a sip of her tea. "Could you be analyzing a little?"

"I'm sorry, that's not my place, but I don't think it's possible for anyone to judge what's best for anyone else. Brent and Krista made their decision a long time ago."

"They never really formulated the plans until you came along with the *Wedding* magazine bribery—"

"Bribery? They read the magazine, they entered the contest, and they won. That's all there was to it."

"The hoopla was very tempting. People get married every day, hundreds of them. Very few get their wedding on the cover of a national magazine with everything first-class and everything paid for. Brent and Krista could have gone on for months, years, without setting a date. Eventually, they would have realized their mistake. I believe that absolutely, and so does Matt. You changed everything."

"Brent and Krista are all grown up, Suzanne. I'm afraid that's a fact you and Matt can't quite face. They're getting married, and they're under enough pressure with the wedding coming up. I think it's wrong for the two people they love best in the world to be against them."

"You're a tough one, Molly. I like that, but obviously you have a stake in this, too. It wouldn't be convenient for *Wedding* if they decided to cancel their plans. But I can see you also fight for what you believe in, and it looks like you believe in this marriage."

Molly felt a momentary twinge of uncertainty, which she quickly dismissed.

"So I'll lay off. Now, tell me about the plans."

Molly got up, poured them both another cup of tea, and brought the wedding catalog to the table.

Suzanne studied the bridal gown carefully. "Hmm."

Molly waited.

"I'd expected something a little simpler."

"It's Victorian."

"Well, I can picture Krista in an old-fashioned dress, but not one quite so . . . flouncy."

"We wanted something that would complement this glorious old house, and Victorian seemed perfect. Krista will be stunning."

"Everything looks lovely on her. But a simple cotton dress, straight, with maybe a little embroidery and old lace. . . . Am I still living in the sixties?"

"Possibly, and that style is fine, but not for this wedding, and certainly not for the magazine."

Molly didn't catch herself in time to leave the magazine out of the conversation, but Suzanne refrained from responding. They were at odds but not at each other's throat. Yet.

There was another subject to be broached.

"About your dress . . ." Molly began carefully.

"You'd like for it to be something in tune with the wedding theme?"

She nodded. "The bridesmaids will also wear Victorian-style dresses, lilac colored . . ."

"Hmm."

"Something pastel might be appropriate."

"I'm afraid not."

"Then what would you like, Suzanne?" Molly gritted her teeth.

"A floral print, maybe jungle green and hot pink."

Molly suppressed a grimace.

"I wear a lot of silver."

"Yes, I was admiring your accessories."

"Most of them are Native American, from the mideighteen hundreds. They look very nice with floral colors. Bright vibrant colors," she added deliberately.

She wasn't going to cooperate, and there was nothing Molly could do about it. If the dress was atrocious, she'd just tell Pete to shoot around Suzanne. "Anything you want is fine," Molly said, defeated.

Suzanne got to her feet. "I'm so glad we had this chat."

"Me, too. And the tea was delicious."

"Krista can use the herbs in her cooking. She does a lot of French dishes, you know."

With that she was gone, leaving Molly to hover over her notebook. Slowly and methodically she checked her lists, as if by keeping the wedding in order on paper, she could handle a situation that seemed to be going dangerously out of control.

6

Molly put the car into first gear and bucked across the intersection. She'd been using Krista's sports car for two days but still wasn't used to a stick shift. She didn't own a car herself, and when she visited Vermont she drove her mother's automatic. Getting used to changing gears on the steep streets of Dillard had been a challenge. Only one of many, Molly reminded herself.

The dresses had arrived on schedule, and Krista was being fitted while Molly went for one more trip to the caterer. She'd finally settled on a menu she liked, although it was terribly impractical and ridiculously expensive. But it was classy and opulent, which is exactly what she wanted for the wedding. Lobster Newburg, wild rice and fresh fruit, or as close to fresh as possible in March. She wanted asparagus, too, for added color, the presentation of the food being utmost in Molly's mind. She'd convinced the caterer to see if he could get it flown in from California.

In fact, she'd done a lot of convincing with the caterer, called Splendiferous Eats, a name that made her cringe. In spite of that, she'd worked out a deal that included a cut-rate charge in exchange for free publicity in *Wedding*.

"You win, we win," Molly had told the owner with a knowing smile. He'd put up a stubborn front before acquiescing but Molly knew he wouldn't have given up the chance for the world. Splendiferous Eats would be the talk of Dillard and the entire surrounding area. And Molly would save the magazine a great deal of money. It was one of her better coups, and she had to pat herself on the back. Molly was the first to admit that she liked to be on the winning side.

Most of the loose ends and details had been taken care of with similar ease. Even Matt Kincaid. He'd been noticeably absent from the house, off on a two-day skiing trip arranged through Kincaid Ltd. Molly caught herself wondering about the skiing party. She had no doubt he would have organized a group that included plenty of young women—gorgeous and appropriately worshipful. They wouldn't be hard to find in Dillard where Matt was the local hero. But whoever he was with, it was none of her business. Besides, with him gone, she'd have no distractions from the wedding plans.

SHE PULLED INTO the Kincaid driveway and stepped on the brake, forgetting all about the clutch. The car choked immediately and shuddered to a stop. Molly shrugged. No problem. She was where she wanted to be.

Then she noticed the other car parked in the driveway. They weren't expecting out-of-town guests, especially not anyone driving a beat-up Jeep with Texas plates. It would have to be the elusive Pete Walenski.

Molly ran up the steps and into the front hall. He was lying on the living-room sofa, hands behind his head, apparently sound asleep. In his well-worn leather jacket, jeans and T-shirt, he looked comfortably at-home. The door slammed behind her, and Pete opened an eye.

"I knew it was you, Molly. No one else charges into a room like that." He sat up, brushed his straight black hair from his forehead and got to his feet, stretching to his full six foot three inches. "Come on, babe, give me a hug."

"I ought to give you a tongue-lashing," she answered, before getting caught in his bear hug. "Where the hell have you been?"

Pete looked down at her, his brown eyes dancing. "Well, let's see. In January, I was in Ethiopia, and before that—"

"I don't need the history of your exotic assignments, Pete."

"You asked—"

"Where have you been for the past few days?"

"Oh, that."

"Yes, that." She extracted herself from his embrace.

"I lost the Harley in Houston and decided to pick up a Jeep. I always wanted one."

"You could have called. I wasn't sure you'd even make it for the wedding."

"Molly, babe, you know I never miss an assignment. What's the rush about these nuptials? We've got time."

"Just enough, Pete, *babe.* I want photos of the pre-wedding festivities. The showers, bachelor parties, dances, luncheons."

"I know the whole gig, Molly, and we're still six days away from the main event."

"This one's going to require a lot more work. I want a whole atmospheric kind of thing—" Molly gestured broadly. "The house, the town, the surrounding mountains. And I want shots of Krista in her wedding gown. Did you meet her?"

"Who?"

"Krista. The bride." Molly raised an eyebrow. "How'd you get in?"

"I rang the doorbell. Someone called down from upstairs and told me to come on in. Haven't seen the blushing bride, or anyone else." Pete shrugged and settled his long lanky frame back on the sofa. "'Course, if you've seen one, you've seen them all."

"Don't be sarcastic, Pete. Krista is . . . Well, she's special."

"Sure, sure. Small-town babe who's finally caught a guy."

"Krista is a lovely young woman and her fiancé is a fine young man."

Pete looked heavenward. "You're lecturing, Molly."

"Well, you're just going to have to listen," she ordered, smiling. "I just don't think you should be so quick to put down small towns. I know Dillard isn't Rome or Budapest or—"

"Or Beirut. That's where I was most recently on assignment."

Molly cocked her head. "Then I'm surprised that you're here and in one piece."

"If I weren't so shy, I'd show you my scar. Got caught in a little cross fire. That's the reason I came back. Decided I needed some R and R, so I flew back to the States. I got bored hanging around my apartment though, so I told my agent to find me something, even a wedding—"

"Which pays as well as your more dangerous assignments, I might add."

"No argument there. Work is work and I wanted to work. I'm addicted. You know that."

Molly understood. Pete was as driven by his career as she was by hers. He practically vibrated with energy and vitality. Even without cameras slung around his neck, Pete's brown eyes constantly took in the scenes around him, lining up shots.

Molly sat down beside him. "I'm really glad we could get you, Pete, in spite of my lectures. I'm determined to make this more than the usual run-of-the mill sweet and syrupy layout. This young couple's wedding is going to be lavish and sophisticated, with an old-fashioned touch that you'll be able to capture for me. Just look at this house—"

"I've already done some prowling."

"No surprise," Molly said dryly.

"Great textures in the oak woodwork and wainscoting. The staircase has a sweeping *Gone With the Wind* look. If I can get up high—"

"You'll think of a way. We could win some awards with this one, and it won't be a puff piece. I'm aiming for at least ten pages."

Pete whistled. "Going for broke, huh?"

"You bet. It has potential."

"Now if this Kathy babe is—"

"Krista," Molly corrected.

"If this Krista babe is anywhere near a ten—"

There was a rustle on the stairway landing. Molly grabbed Pete's hand and pulled him into the hall.

They looked up and caught their breaths at the same time. Diffused rays of sunlight falling through the stained-glass skylight bathed Krista in a rainbow of color. In her wedding dress, she looked both radiant and ethereal.

Pete and Molly stood in stunned silence.

"I'm not a perfect size eight after all," Krista said. "The dress is pinned up but I thought you might want to see how it looks." She spoke shyly. "Is it okay for me to come down?"

Molly had made a mistake and she knew it. She never should have pulled Pete out into the hall. Her first instinct was to tell Krista to go back where she came from. Before she could speak, Pete answered.

"No, don't come down. Let me come up to you."

Molly reached out to stop him but failed to get a firm hold on his jacket as he brushed by her and took the steps two at a time.

Krista stood waiting. When Pete reached her, Molly's mouth fell open as she watched what he did. Dropping to his knees, he took one of Krista's hands in his. The expression on his face raised goose bumps on the back of Molly's neck. He looked like a man who'd been hit by a bolt of lighting.

He raised Krista's hand to his lips. *"Ma belle dame sans merci . . ."*

Molly didn't know whether to laugh or cry.

Pete's eyes locked with Krista's, and Molly realized that both of them had forgotten she was alive. She leaned weakly against the banister and looked helplessly at the tableau above her.

Pete knelt at Krista's feet like a Knight of the Round Table pledging his loyalty and love to his lady. Except Pete was a knight in blue jeans, and Krista was someone else's bride.

Regaining her composure, Molly surged into action. She flew up the stairs and pulled Krista's hand away from Pete. They both looked at her with dazed eyes. "Krista, this is our photographer, Pete Walenski. Pete, this is Krista. Now that you've been introduced, I think you should go back up and change, Krista."

"Don't you want to look at the dress?" she asked distractedly. "You told me we needed to see how it moved—"

"Of course. Allow me." Pete took Krista's arm and ushered her down the stairs. Side by side, they moved majestically, as if on their way to a coronation. Like a robot, Molly followed.

Pete deposited Krista in the middle of the hall and began to circle her, not saying a word, just looking. Molly had once heard the expression, drinking her in with his eyes. Now she was seeing it. Pete was behaving like a love-starved teenager, and Krista was lapping it up.

As for Molly, she was scared, damned scared. Something was happening right in front of her and she was powerless to stop it. There was a spark in the air. It had been missing between Krista and Brent, and suddenly Molly realized that's what had worried her from the beginning. The excitement she'd longed for to make the wedding perfect was here and now. And Brent was nowhere to be seen.

"Is she magnificent or what?" Pete asked.

"She's lovely," Molly managed to choke out. Krista beamed as the dress swirled around her, its long train flowing in satin drapes from the bustle. It was the perfect choice, Molly told herself. Under any other circumstances that would have made her ecstatic. But she couldn't let her dismay show. For now, she'd just have to ignore what was going on and try not to make a big deal about Pete and Krista.

"The bodice is elegant, don't you think, Molly?" Krista was talking to Molly but looking at Pete, who was certainly not unaware of the bodice, Molly suspected.

It was beaded with tiny seed pearls and hugged Krista like a glove. The neck was high and banded with more lace, and the sleeves puffed at the shoulders and tapered to arm-hugging lace from Krista's elbow to her wrist. She'd even put on the veil, which was held in place with delicate white flowers and more seed pearls. It cascaded around her face like foam from the sea.

"Oh, thank you, Molly," Krista said softly. "Thank you."

Molly looked at her sharply, frowning.

"For the dress," Krista added.

"Oh, yes, well, you need to go up and take it off right now. Immediately. It might get dirty—"

"Not yet," Pete interrupted. "Let me get my cameras."

"No," Molly burst out. She knew her voice was high-pitched and strained. She tried to calm herself as much as possible and aimed for a logical response. "That won't be necessary. It's only pinned, and the seamstress is waiting for it. Krista probably needs to leave—or something," she finished lamely.

"I guess you're right." Krista's face had a soft, dreamy look. She smiled at Pete. "Will you be staying with us?"

"Yes," he said immediately.

"No," Molly corrected. "I've booked a room at the Dillard Inn. The bridesmaids will need the extra room to dress in." She glowered at Pete.

He shrugged and kept looking at Krista.

"Then will you come for dinner? My brother gets home tonight. And my fiancé will be here," she added, almost as an afterthought.

"Sounds good to me."

It didn't sound good to Molly. "Pete, you and I need to have dinner tonight and talk business."

"We can talk in the morning, Molly," he said breezily. Of course he was right. There was nothing that couldn't wait. Nothing pertaining to business, anyway.

Krista beamed. "Then we'll see you tonight about seven."

"I'll be here."

Those should have been his parting words, but Molly noticed that he didn't seem to be going anywhere. Neither did Krista. They continued to stand in the middle of the hall, looking at each other.

Molly'd had enough. "Pete, you go freshen up or whatever men do before dinner, and Krista you go upstairs and get out of that dress, and I'm going to take an aspirin."

Somehow she got them moving—Pete out the door, Krista up the stairs. Then she dug around in her purse and found the aspirin bottle. She went into the kitchen and took two.

Six days until the wedding, and anything could happen.

MATT STOOD QUIETLY in the kitchen doorway, so he wouldn't make his presence known. He liked watching Molly when she didn't know he was around. He liked the way she moved, quickly but with grave deliberation. He liked the way she looked in jeans—a small neat package, nicely rounded. And he liked her hair, its curls almost uncontrollable today. She brushed them back with a gesture that was delightfully feminine. It made him smile. When she didn't know anyone was looking, Molly Prescott was almost adorable.

She stood at the kitchen stove and poked experimentally at something simmering in a large Dutch oven. She looked worried, he thought, and that raised his spirits. Maybe her perfect wedding plans were falling apart.

Matt stepped into the kitchen and sniffed. "Smells great. Didn't know you could cook, Prescott. A woman of many talents."

She put the top back on the pot. "I can cook, but I don't, not often anyway. Your sister fixed this. Beef bourguignon. We're having company for dinner."

"Who? Besides Brent, who's always around at mealtime." He sauntered over to the stove, lifted the lid and decided the meat looked as good as it smelled.

"My photographer from New York. Pete Walenski. He arrived today."

Matt wasn't particularly interested in the photographer. He was more interested in what was going on with Molly. She seemed on edge. "Is the guy a problem, or what?"

"He's one of the best photographers in the country. In the world, in fact. There're absolutely no problems."

Matt bit back a smile. With Prescott on the defensive, he knew something was up. "Is this guy an ex-lover of yours? Is that why you're so upset? Or maybe a current lover?"

"I'm not upset. And he's not a lover—current or otherwise. Pete is a co-worker and a friend."

He thought she was going to say something more about the wedding, but she changed the subject abruptly as she often did when the topic became too uncomfortable.

"How was the skiing trip? Did all the little snow bunnies have a good time?"

Matt took the wooden spoon from her and tasted the stew. "Delicious." He gave the spoon back. "Now, about those snow bunnies. They consist of five couples in their sixties who make the trip every year with their kids and grandkids. Krista usually goes along to give lessons and act as troubleshooter. Since she's involved with the famous Wedding of the Month, I took her place."

"Oh," Molly said in a chastised tone.

"Krista is really a better skier than I am," he admitted. "Strong, steady, sure of herself. I was always too much of a hotshot." He noticed that she didn't look the least bit surprised by that. "I liked to take chances. Used to get thrown off the slopes pretty often."

"Figures." Molly rinsed off the spoon and gave it back to him. "Watch over it for me, will you? I need to go up and talk to Krista."

"Prescott, are you sure there isn't a problem?"

"Sorry to disappoint you, Kincaid. Everything is perfect. The wedding will go on as planned." She marched toward the door and then turned back to look at him. "Just watch the stew, and don't try to stir up anything else."

Matt turned back to the stove and dipped the spoon in the bubbling stew. "Prescott, honey," he said when she was safely out of earshot, "I'm not going to have to stir up anything but this stew. The trouble's already here."

TROUBLE WAS ON Molly's mind as she reached the top of the stairs. Did Matt know? Impossible. Did he suspect? Likely. He'd probably put two and two together and decided something had happened between Pete and Krista. But nothing *had* happened, Molly told herself. It was all in her imagination.

She knocked on Krista's door. "It's Molly. Can I come in?"

"Sure. It's open."

Krista was sitting at her dressing table putting on earrings. Molly looked at her closely. She seemed to be back to her old self, which caused Molly to relax a little.

"How's the stew?" Krista asked.

"Your brother is home. I put him in charge."

"Great." Krista picked up her brush and ran it through her long blond hair. "Let's be casual tonight." She was dressed in wool pants and a sweater. "I'll wear this." She looked up at Molly's reflection in the mirror. "You don't need to change out of your jeans."

"Good idea."

"I think the guys will feel more comfortable if we don't dress up."

"You're probably right." Molly couldn't wait around much longer. If Krista didn't mention Pete, she'd have to.

"Did I tell Pete seven o'clock?"

Finally. Molly nodded and then took advantage of the opening. "What did you think about the peripatetic photographer?" she asked, trying to keep her question casual.

"He's fun. It's going to be great working with him. What a sense of humor."

Molly felt the tension drain out of her shoulders and neck. Not sexy, fascinating or compelling. Just fun. "You think he's amusing?"

Krista turned on the stool to face Molly. "Sure, don't you? The way he carried on when he saw me in the wedding dress—it was like something out of an old movie! I was flattered, of course, but I knew it was a joke."

Molly didn't know any such thing, but she was very willing to agree. "Yes, he's quite a joker."

"And if he's half the photographer you say—"

"Oh, no doubt about that."

"Then we'll have the best wedding pictures ever."

Molly pulled Krista to her feet. "That I'll promise. Now, let's get this show on the road. I may not be much of a cook, but my salads are legendary."

"Great. Dinner tonight will give Pete something to make him sit up and take notice."

Without allowing herself to wonder what had brought on that remark, Molly headed toward the bedroom door, with Krista in tow.

She couldn't keep from thinking about it, however, and it was still on her mind when Pete and Brent arrived—at almost the same time. She held her breath through the introductions as the two men acknowledged each other politely. Then she sighed in relief when Pete recognized Matt, a fellow world traveler and adventurer.

Matt turned on the charm for the photographer. He even went into his wine reserve and brought out two special bottles of red he'd been saving. The wine flowed all around, and while Matt and Pete talked about mountaineering, Molly led Krista and Brent into a discussion about an upcoming party.

Krista and Pete had spoken only briefly and casually. Everything was fine. Then why, Molly wondered, did she still feel on edge, as if something dreadful was about to happen?

About eight o'clock the party moved from the living room into the kitchen. "We're really casual tonight," Krista declared, "so Molly and I decided not to set the dining-room table. Sit down, everyone. We've got a real treat."

They all obliged. Matt topped off all the wine glasses, and with a flourish Krista put the Dutch oven on the table and lifted the lid.

"Beef stew," Brent said. "My favorite."

"*Boeuf bourguignon*," Pete announced. "*C'est mon favori, aussi.*"

Molly gulped hard. The evening that had begun so well was beginning to go downhill.

PETE AND KRISTA CHATTED in French while the stew was being served. Molly caught a few words and understood that the subject was food, but she couldn't follow the conversation. Matt threw in a phrase now and then, but Brent seemed totally lost.

Molly rushed to the rescue. "All right, you guys, let Brent and me in on the conversation. Our French is a little rusty."

"Molly, I don't know about Brent, but your French is nonexistent," Pete corrected.

Molly shrugged, relieved that she was taking the brunt of the teasing. "*Je suis une Américaine.*"

"We're all Americans, Molly," Pete said with a grin. "Some of us are just a little more worldly." It was clearly a joke, but Molly couldn't tell how Brent took it.

"So translate," she prodded.

"We were talking about a bistro on the Left Bank in Paris. It turns out Krista and I both had dinner there. Isn't it funny that we'd search out the same little café?"

"Quite a coincidence."

"It gets even better," Krista added. "We both had the *boeuf bourguignon!*"

"Not as good as this—but good," Pete complimented.

"Well, I haven't eaten it anywhere else," Brent cut in, "but Krista's is good enough for me." He gave her a quick, possessive kiss that Molly hoped would set things straight.

She ate her stew and waited. The kiss didn't seem to stop Pete, who continued to compare notes with Krista about Paris. But at least he'd decided to speak in English.

Matt was warming to the conversation. "Let's see if we can make this small world even smaller. Have you been to Delhi, Pete?"

"More than once."

"There's a great hotel, the Wellington, with a great bar—"

"The Waterloo," Pete finished. "One of my favorite spots."

"I didn't know there were mountains in Delhi," Molly said suspiciously. She wondered if Matt was putting them on.

"I was on my way to Nepal."

"Yeah, I always stop off in Delhi on my way to Nepal," Brent cracked.

Molly threw Brent a sympathetic look. His remark was pleasant enough, but she could tell he was getting irritated. It was time for the world travelers to lay off.

But Pete and Matt were deep in conversation again, comparing countries and restaurants and recalling funny little cafés where they'd had the best meals of their lives.

Molly was beginning to wonder about their motives. Pete had a thing for Krista—that was obvious. And Matt objected to the wedding—also obvious. It was as if they'd compared notes and decided to go for it. Krista had joined right in, completely oblivious to Brent's discomfort. She was enjoying herself telling anecdotes about the exotic recipes she'd tried, usually at Matt's suggestion, often with disastrous results.

Near the end of the meal, Molly made a determined effort to include Brent. "What kind of food do you like?" she asked.

"Pretty much plain food." He shot a defiant look at Pete.

"Time to explore a little," Pete suggested, "expand your palate."

"My palate's fine. In fact, I imagine we enjoy similar food. We just call it by different names. This *stew* is excellent."

"But you don't like the more exotic recipes, Brent," Krista reminded him.

Molly sank down into her chair. Krista couldn't have made a worse comment.

"Sure I do."

"No, Brent, remember when I made the tabouli?"

"That's not a very good example, Krista."

"It's okay, Brent. I used to be like that," Pete said, "when I was your age."

Molly groaned. Pete, not yet thirty, was playing the sage.

"Well, we are what we eat, you know." Brent said brusquely. "My simple tastes have kept me in good shape, a hundred-and-seventy-five pounds, mostly muscle."

Molly wondered if Brent was going to flex his arm.

"I'm not in such bad shape myself in spite of my culinary tastes," Pete countered. "I could go a round or two."

Beneath the bantering tone of their voices, Molly sensed a threatening undercurrent in their words. She wondered if this was a secret kind of male code that preceded a fistfight.

"Well, as far as food goes, tonight was wonderful," Molly said evasively. "My compliments to the chef." She got up and began to clear the table. "Lots of people enjoy simple food. I certainly do, and in most countries they offer basic fare—like fish and chips or pasta or—"

Her mind went blank.

Matt, who'd been watching the proceedings with a gleam in his eye, reached for the wine. "Refills?"

"Sure," Pete said. "Great year."

"Not me," Brent answered. "It's too dry."

Pete cocked an eyebrow. "I like a crisp, dry wine. You prefer your wine a little sweeter, huh?"

"Yes, in fact," Brent said stiffly.

"No accounting for taste."

"Or for manners," Brent responded.

"Brent!" Krista, who'd been watching the exchange with a deepening frown, tried to intervene. "Pete's our guest."

"That doesn't give him the right to question my taste."

"I didn't say you had *bad* taste," Pete shot back.

"True," Matt threw in.

"And I didn't say you had *bad* manners," Brent responded.

"True again."

Matt was obviously enjoying himself, but a major confrontation was brewing, and Molly wasn't about to let it go any further. She rapped on the side of a pot with her spoon. "I hereby declare this dinner party over. All of us are tired—"

"I'm not," Matt piped in.

"Pete is. He's very tired." She looked long and hard at the photographer, who merely smiled in response.

"Pete is so tired he probably wants to go to his hotel room and get some sleep."

Pete took a sip of his wine. "Well . . ."

"I'll make it easy for you," Brent said roughly, "by leaving first. I *am* tired, tired of all this." He stood up, grabbed his coat and headed for the door.

"Brent—" Krista called after him.

"I'll see you for dinner tomorrow, Krista. Alone." He went out the door and into the night.

Molly saw tears in Krista's eyes. "I don't know what came over Brent, to get that upset about food—" She dabbed at her eyes with her napkin. "He loves that wine. I just don't understand why he was so . . . so contrary. That's not like Brent."

Molly looked at Matt. He winked, letting her know that he was aware the argument hadn't been over food or wine. It was over Krista. Molly's heart sank. What had begun between Krista and Pete on the stairs wasn't over yet. She planned to give him a good talking to.

"Wedding jitters," Molly assured them. "We're all a little on edge."

"I'm not at all on edge," Matt contradicted. "I think Pete has some good points. Brent can be a bit parochial."

Molly opened her mouth to speak.

"Let me finish, Prescott. Pete pointed out some things that I've been saying all along. Brent doesn't know enough about life. It's to be lived, Prescott. And the world is out there to be traveled."

"Hear, hear," Pete chimed in. "Couldn't have put it better myself. I say see the world before settling down."

"You've seen the world, Pete," Molly said, "but you've only been in this town a few hours, so don't pretend to be an expert on Krista and Brent."

"It didn't take you long to become an expert, if I remember correctly," Matt countered. "You had plenty of advice for Krista."

"I'm here to help put on a wedding. It's my job to be an expert. I'm supposed to give advice. It's your job to give the bride away, and Pete's job to take pictures. You both overstepped your bounds tonight."

"Does that mean we can't talk shop, Molly?"

"That wasn't shop. That was show-off."

"Stop it, stop it, all of you." Krista put her hands over her ears. "You're making me crazy."

"Krista—" Matt and Molly spoke at once.

Krista ignored them as she got up. "Everyone seems to know what's right for me. All I ever hear is what I should be doing or wearing or eating. I'm a grown woman! I know what I want, and what I want now is for all of you to butt out and leave me alone. This is my wedding. This is my life." With a strangled sob she whirled and ran from the room, leaving three speechless people behind.

7

PETE REACHED FOR his leather jacket. "Looks like I'm outta here."

Molly watched him shrug into the jacket. "*Now* he says it."

"Molly, don't scold. It isn't becoming."

When she didn't answer, Pete walked over and kissed her on the cheek. "You get what you pay for, babe, and you paid for the best photographer. I know, I know. Unfortunately—she's thinking—the camera comes with a man attached." He laughed, shook Matt's hand and then paused by the back door. "Tell Krista I'm sorry. I just got carried away about being a world traveler. I'll even call Brett—"

"Brent," Molly shouted, "and don't call him, please. Just leave well enough alone."

Pete lifted his hand in a mock salute. "Your wish is my command. Be prepared for my best behavior."

"I'm not only prepared for it, I'm counting on it."

The door closed behind him, and Molly looked over at Matt. "Well, are you satisfied?"

"Whenever a woman asks me that I know I'm in big trouble, even though I never have quite figured out what it means."

"In this case it means you started it, you egged Pete on when you knew perfectly well Brent was feeling left out."

"Life is tough, Prescott. Brent is a big boy, and it's time he stopped running for cover whenever the going gets rough. He needs to learn a few of life's realities."

"Such as?"

"Krista is a beautiful woman. If he wants her, he needs to fight for her."

"Not that again." Molly sank down in a chair.

"Reality, Prescott."

"The reality of this night was very obvious—Pete showing off and Brent getting jealous. Just like children. And you couldn't leave it alone. You had to jump in on Pete's side, still trying to show Krista that the wedding is a big mistake."

"Which it is. Couldn't you tell that tonight? Krista was fascinated by Pete."

"I certainly hope you don't think Pete and Krista—"

"I didn't say that. I wouldn't choose Walenski for my sister, either—"

"Ah," Molly said keenly. "There we have it. *You* want to make the choice for her. Well, you're not in charge of her life."

"Neither are you," Matt shot back.

"I know that." Molly got up abruptly and began stacking the dishes in the sink. "I wasn't the one who—"

"Can't hear you, Prescott. If you're going to talk to me, you'll have to leave the dishes alone."

She turned around. "I said, I wasn't the one who acted as if liking meat and potatoes was a criminal offense. You and Pete were as boorish as Brent was stubborn."

"Well, now that we're getting into it, Krista loves exotic foods and she likes to experiment. Which doesn't quite make it with Brent's meat and potatoes appetite."

"They'll work it out." Molly turned back to the sink.

Matt got up and stood beside her. "Guess I'll have to help with the dishes if I want to hear what you're saying." He reached for the sponge, but she grabbed it first and held tight.

"Don't you want my help?"

"No, thanks." She soaped a dish, rinsed it, and put it in the drainer.

"I'll dry."

"Please, don't bother. I can do it."

"A real take-charge woman. Not exactly my type, but—"

"This isn't about you and me, Matt. It's about Krista and Pete—I mean, Krista and Brent," Molly corrected, but not fast enough. Matt was already laughing.

"See, you aren't even sure who she belongs with." He found a dishcloth and began drying.

"I said I could take care of the dishes."

"The dishes, Krista and Pete—I mean, Krista and Brent. You can take care of everything, can't you, Prescott?"

He finished drying the two dishes she'd put in the drainer and then made a more successful grab for the sponge. "But you're awfully slow."

Before she knew it they were both splashing around in the sink, and soapy water was flying.

"This'll never work," Matt said. "Let me wash, and you can dry."

"Just leave me alone and I'll do both." Molly tried again for the sponge.

"You're too slow—it'll take all night."

"Well, you're too sloppy. Look at this." She held up a dinner plate. "It's not even clean."

"You know what, Prescott? I don't think either of us is very domestic. And you have suds on your cheek." He reached out with the dish towel and dabbed at her cheek, and Molly found herself looking into his eyes, wondering again at their color. Were they blue or gray? It was still impossible to tell. But whatever the color, she didn't intend to get lost in them this time.

"This is ridiculous," Molly said, shaking her head. "We're down here splashing around in the sink while Krista's upstairs crying. One of us should talk to her."

"I will," Matt volunteered. "Krista never has liked controversy. Maybe she can avoid it by reconsidering the whole wedding thing—"

Molly handed him the sponge. "In that case, I'll talk to her. She needs a kind word, not another lecture."

Matt gave the sponge back. "I'll do it, and I won't lecture."

"Do you promise?"

"My word as a dishwasher." Matt headed toward the hall.

"Just listen for a change," Molly called after him.

"I will if you will, Prescott."

He was up the stairs before she could answer.

MATT DID AS HE WAS told. He would have anyway; this wasn't the time to upset Krista further. So he comforted her, assured her everything was going to be all right. And then she extracted a promise from him.

"Will you do something for me, Matt?" Krista asked through her tears.

"Anything, Kristabel."

"Try to get along with Molly."

"We get along . . . kind of."

"I know you're teasing, but if you and Molly could quit arguing it would lower the stress level on me about a thousand percent. Do something nice for her, Matt. Take her to dinner up in the mountains. Take her to the Timberline Inn and make things better."

Matt agreed, but he didn't tell his sister that he'd already decided it was time to take Molly to his favorite Colorado restaurant. Dinner at the Timberline was exactly what he'd had in mind.

AFTER MUCH PERSUASION, Molly agreed to a date for the next night. When they were halfway up the mountain, it started to snow.

"We'd better turn around," Molly advised.

"What?" Matt had been thinking about the evening ahead, fantasizing a little, he admitted to himself, about

Molly sitting across the table from him, candlelight dancing in her wild crazy hair. The problem was he couldn't even finish a fantasy without Molly giving him orders.

"Turn back. It's snowing."

Matt just laughed. "We're almost there, Prescott, and a little snow is just what we need to make the evening perfect. A romantic fireside table, a bottle of good wine, snow falling all around, city lights flickering below. The view's spectacular."

"It's the snow falling all around part that worries me. Suppose we get stuck in it?"

"You're talking to the driver of Colorado's most adventurous vehicle. The four-wheel-drive Matt-mobile goes anywhere man has ever ventured and then some." Matt patted the dashboard. "Besides, even if the snow continues, there won't be any accumulation to speak of for hours. We're fine, Prescott. Don't worry."

Molly sat back and tried to take his advice. Matt's mind was made up, and she knew it was pointless to argue. She'd just have to try enjoying herself and hope he was right.

By the time they reached the inn, Molly was still worried, but she put on a brave front.

Matt angled into the parking lot, turned off the engine and looked over at her. "Okay, Prescott, for the first half of the drive you gave me your play-by-play of the wedding—why Krista and Brent are meant to be together, and why I'm so opinionated."

"I—"

"Let me finish. For the last half you pouted because it's snowing. I propose we decree that the wedding and the snow are both taboo for the rest of the evening."

Molly shrugged. "Okay. But what does that leave us to talk about?"

Matt laughed and got out of the car. As he opened Molly's door, he said thoughtfully, "You and I should have a lot to talk about since we're so much alike."

"Alike?" She looked at him, dumbfounded.

"I'll explain later." Matt took her arm and led her up the broad steps of the inn. "I have another suggestion. We could just try to enjoy ourselves."

Molly teased him back. "Enjoy ourselves? You and me? Impossible, Kincaid. But," she added as they stepped into the lobby, "I'll give it a shot."

Matt was well-known at the Timberline Inn, Molly wasn't surprised to learn. The desk clerk waved to him, the manager made a special point of saying hello and the hostess in the very crowded restaurant led them to Matt's special table.

The room was big and cozy, with dark paneling, high beamed ceilings and wide picture windows that looked out on the city far below. Fires roared in the two large fireplaces at opposite ends of the restaurant, and the scent of the pine logs permeated the room. Molly was enchanted.

"You like it, don't you, Prescott?"

"I certainly do. So far," she added. "If the food equals the ambience..."

"Far surpasses it. I'll order for you." He reached for her menu.

"Now wait a minute—"

"Come on, Prescott, I know the place. You can't always be the boss."

"Always?" Molly was incredulous, but she caught the glimmer in his eye, laughed and turned over the menu to him. "Can I trust you?"

"Count on it."

He ordered wine from the hovering waiter and then chose steak for their entreé.

"I'd really prefer fish. Maybe mountain trout?"

"You object to my choice?"

"Not an objection. Just a preference."

"Well, it's too early in the season for trout, Prescott. You're in Colorado, remember. Try the steak. It won't be like any you've ever eaten. It's all in the way the meat is grilled. I told you, trust me."

Molly went along with his choice. She loved to eat and above all loved to eat good food. It didn't surprise her that the steak turned out to be delicious, the bread hot and crusty, the vegetables fresh and crisp.

She looked across the table at Matt after tasting some of everything. "I feel relaxed for the first time in ages. I'm really enjoying myself."

"In spite of the snow."

It was still coming down hard, but it was also beautiful, blanketing the dark and shadowy pines just outside the windows. "It's very peaceful, actually."

"You're getting the spirit. Of course, it could be the wine and food."

"And the fact that, although we argued just a little bit over your choice of entrée, we haven't gotten into a shouting match."

"Yet," Matt added with a grin.

"But then we never would fight if—as you said—we were so much alike. Which we aren't. I'm not out climbing mountains." She cocked an eyebrow at him. "By the way, you never told me how you got into that."

"Into what?"

"Mountain climbing, Kincaid. That's what we're talking about."

"I thought the subject was how much we're alike, but I'll digress for a moment. I got into climbing at summer camp when I was in college. I was the assistant counselor for mountain sports, and since there was no snow, we had to climb. I turned out to be pretty good so the next summer I joined a climbing club. After graduation, my parents sent me to Europe and I climbed in Switzerland."

"The Matterhorn." Molly was pleased to come up with the name of a mountain and place it in the right country.

"Among others. It was quite a summer." He grinned. "I found out two things. First, that girls think mountain climbers are daring and sexy."

"Well, I'm stunned that you'd admit that."

"As usual you underestimate me. I'm always honest, about myself and other people."

Molly sipped at the wine, which was an excellent choice. "What was the other thing you learned?"

"That I needed money to spend my life scaling mountains. I talked Dad into letting me run the store and expand it to appeal to a younger crowd. The place took off, Dad retired, Krista came into the business—"

"And the rest is history."

"Something like that. The mountain climber image still impresses women. With one exception." Matt touched his wineglass to hers. "The wine impressed you, though."

"Yes."

"And the steak."

"Very much. In fact, everything—"

"But the mountain climber."

"Maybe I don't fit the groupie profile, but I think your career is interesting."

"Not romantic?"

Molly shook her head.

"Not sexy?"

"Not in the slightest." Molly turned serious. "What matters is that you love what you do."

"Absolutely. And it has everything to do with the experience, nothing to do with impressing women. The secret valleys of Tibet filled with pink flowers, dawn along the Hindu Kush, or sunset on Annapurna when the snow reflects red as blood and you can hear the wind sweeping down Nanda Devi." His words were mysterious and mystical, conjuring up the romance of faraway places.

"You sound like a poet, Matt." That surprised her and brought on a sudden rush of tenderness toward him. It also might have been what caused her to call him by his first name again.

"Mountain climbers tend to get poetic when they talk about an expedition, I guess. I know one thing, I'll never give this life up, even if I have to be pushed up the mountain in a wheelchair."

"I admire you for that. You're lucky to love what you do."

He studied her face intently. "Am I to read into your remark that you don't love what you do? Is there less than perfect bliss at *Wedding*?"

"I'm not sure bliss is the word—or should be."

"It's a good word, though."

Molly could see where he was leading. Matt was alluding to sex. As usual. "It's out of context here."

Matt shrugged. "Then if not blissful, is it wonderful?"

"Well, let's say I like my work very much, or most things about it. Nothing is a hundred-percent perfect."

"What do you like most about it?"

Molly looked at him suspiciously.

"I'm interested, Prescott."

Taking a chance that he really was, she answered. "I like being in charge, running the show. I like making the decisions that reflect my taste and talent. The decisions that count."

The hint of a smile quirked the corners of Matt's mouth. "Were you a bossy little girl, too?"

Molly was on the verge of being offended. Then she laughed. "Yes, I admit to having been a horribly bossy little girl. My younger brother and sister bore the brunt of it. I made them play my games, my way."

Matt finished his wine. "So you see, we're more alike than you thought. I was a bossy kid, too. I still like to be in charge and have everything my way. We'd make an interesting team if we ever got on the same side." Matt paused and looked at her so directly she felt herself blushing under his gaze. "I like a woman who knows what she wants."

Molly couldn't continue to meet his eyes. The look in them made her warm all over. More than warm, it made her hot. She held the cool wineglass against her cheek and sneaked another look at him, avoiding his eyes this time.

She'd noticed earlier that he wore jeans and boots as usual. But tonight he'd varied his wardrobe with a dark shirt open at the neck and a tweed jacket, expensive and well-worn. He was by far the best-looking man in the room, which pleased and annoyed Molly at the same time. She enjoyed being in the company of such a handsome man; on the other hand, no one should be that good-looking. It would be fuel to his self-confidence.

"Do you think it'll ever happen—that we'll be on the same side?" he asked lazily.

"If you change your mind about the wed—" She broke off in mid-word. "Sorry. I forgot the rules."

"You're forgiven." He pushed away his plate and lounged back in his chair. "Let's hear how the bossy little girl grew up to become a self-assured young woman."

"It began with an uneventful childhood and yearnings to leave the small town for the big city."

"Even with all those mountains around you in Vermont."

"I told you I didn't like skiing. I liked to read and write, sit in my room, look out the window and watch the seasons change."

There was a dreamy expression on her face as she remembered. Matt thought how much she fit right into his fantasy. She'd tried to control her wild hair by pinning it up, but as usual some tendrils had resisted and curled around her face. She was wearing a white silk blouse and tiny pearl earrings. It was a very efficient look—a look that tried to be businesslike. Yet despite her aura of self-assurance, the look was also a little vulnerable and terribly sexy.

He thought he saw a faint tremor on her lips and imagined kissing it away. He'd kissed her once, but that hadn't really counted. She'd been caught off guard and had only let herself return the kiss for an instant. But it'd been a great instant. He'd like to try it again, to really kiss her and have her return it. The thought stayed with him while he continued to ask her questions.

"What did you write?"

"Oh, I don't know. Stories about animals, I think."

"Not about your dolls' weddings?"

The mouth lost its vulnerability in a flash. "Couldn't resist, could you, Kincaid? Is this all a tease?"

"No," he said honestly. "I want to know all about you. What were your fantasies?"

"Traveling, getting away from the hometown life. Which I finally did. After college, I went to New York to seek fame and fortune."

"And you say you're not a risk taker. That was quite a big step."

"I knew I wanted to write. When the job at *Wedding* came along, I took it, and I've been happy there. Of course my career never was as exciting or dangerous as climbing mountains—until I met the Kincaids, that is."

Matt figured that jibe made them even and ignored it. "No men in your life out of all those millions in New York City?"

"I've had a couple of semi-serious romances."

"What exactly does that mean?"

"More serious than just dating, less serious than living together."

Matt nodded. "Yeah, I've had a couple of those, too."

The table had been cleared, and the waiter hovered nearby. Matt didn't want the evening to end. "How about dessert and coffee?"

"How about the snow?"

"You want snow for dessert?"

"Matt—"

"All right, all right. Even though you broke the rules by mentioning it, I'll set your mind at ease." He motioned to the waiter. "Ed, tell the lady we're not going to get stuck in the snow. Tell her it's safe to stay for dessert and coffee."

"The snow is no problem, ma'am. Mr. Kincaid has a four-wheel drive, and he can pull right out of here. This is Colorado, after all. It snows a lot."

"See. What did I tell you?" He reached for her hand to reassure her and didn't let go even after she seemed to settle down. "I recommend the double-chocolate cheesecake."

"Well . . ."

"Two cheesecakes, Ed."

Matt was still holding her hand. It was soft and small, almost fragile in his. He liked holding it a lot.

"I guess a few more minutes won't matter," Molly conceded.

THE MINUTES TURNED into an hour. Matt insisted they go into the lounge where a jazz combo was playing, and when she heard the music, old standards from the forties, Molly was seduced. "I love these songs."

"See? Another thing we have in common."

They ordered cappuccino and sat near the window. The snow was still coming down, and every now and then Molly leaned forward and looked out.

"Relax, Prescott. Nothing short of an avalanche would keep me from getting you home. Meantime, how about a dance?"

Molly wasn't quite sure why she decided to dance with him when she knew full well it would be a mistake. But some things just couldn't be explained, she decided as she stepped into his arms and he held her close. The music was soft and low, sweet and romantic, all the things she'd meant to avoid with him.

He'd placed one hand securely against the small of her back; the other held her hand in a warm grasp. Nothing unusual about that, Molly told herself. It was the way men and women danced, after all. Molly thought about the last time she'd been dancing, not that long ago, really. Her date had held her just like this, resting his cheek against her forehead as Matt did now. But it hadn't been the same. She hadn't fit so perfectly.

The song had just begun, and there was nothing she could do now but hope that it would end before something happened. But that something was already happening. She wasn't just in his arms; she was meshed to him, her breasts against his chest, hips and thighs close, much too close.

He was a good dancer. If his dancing was the only issue, everything would have been all right. But it wasn't. Matt wasn't just dancing—he was coming seriously close to making love to her on the dance floor. He moved his hand slowly up her back, caressing her skin through the thin silk material and pulling her closer. Then he dropped her hand and put his other arm around her, holding her in his embrace but still moving languidly, not really dancing, just swaying to the music.

Molly felt a tingle of electricity run through her. She tried to control it but without success. The feeling took over. She was beginning to give in to it when the music ended. The spell broke.

Matt still held her, his lips inches from hers. She turned her head away, stepped out of his arms and moved back toward their table.

A couple had sat down in a booth next to them. Oblivious to Matt and Molly they were lost in a long, lingering kiss. Molly felt her face flush when she saw them, yet she couldn't stop watching. Nor could she control the stirrings of unrest inside her that had begun on the dance floor. It wasn't safe to have such feelings with Matt Kincaid standing just behind her, his hand at her waist.

Molly made up her mind. She wasn't going to sit back down.

"Matt, I really think it's time to go. I have an early day tomorrow, lots of things to do. Besides, the snow—"

"There you go. Talking about snow again," Matt chastised.

"There's no way to avoid it. It's still snowing, Matt, and I don't want to take any chances."

He didn't respond.

"Matt," she said firmly. "I want to go."

Matt glanced at the couple in the booth. "Does romance bother you, Prescott?"

"Don't be ridiculous." She reached for her handbag, without looking at the young couple again, and tried not to think about the dance that had just ended.

As Molly headed toward the door, Matt followed without further comment.

They crossed the lobby and walked to the car in silence. The snow was coming down harder. Molly sighed in relief as Matt started up and pulled out of his parking space. The snow was thick on the ground, but the tires grabbed the surface, and he backed up without skidding. Molly felt confident. The dancing was over; they were on the way back to Dillard. In no time at all, she'd be in bed asleep and thoughts of Matt would be entirely forgotten.

Molly saw the hotel manager before Matt did and touched his arm. "He's waving at us to stop, I think. What could be wrong?" Molly felt her stomach churn.

"Probably forgot something." Matt rolled down the window.

"We've got a problem, Matt."

"The snow," Molly said immediately. "I knew it. We're snowed in."

"Obviously, we're not snowed in, Molly," Matt said with irritation. "What is it, Rusty?"

"There's a tree across the road down about a mile. One of our guests called from below to say they're heading back to Dillard. If they can't get up, I'm afraid you folks can't get down."

"When will it be cleared away?" Molly asked.

"The county should send someone out first thing in the morning."

"In the morning! You mean we're stuck here?"

"I hope you have a couple of rooms for us, Rusty."

"The inn's all booked up—"

"I don't believe this," Molly grumbled.

"But one of the chalets is empty. Guests are coming in tomorrow so you can have it 'til then," he offered.

"One chalet," Molly muttered under her breath. "Just one?"

"It has two bedrooms," the manager explained. "It's our executive chalet. I think you'll find it very nice."

"I'm sure we will, Rusty."

"What about all the other people who can't get home?" Molly asked.

"Everyone who came up from town for dinner left a while back. I reckon the tree went down in the last half hour or so."

Molly gave Matt a withering glance that clearly said they should have left when she suggested.

The look seemed to prompt him to make one final request of the manager. "Give the county boys a nudge, Rusty, and who knows, they might get up here sooner than you expect. If they do, call us. The lady doesn't seem in the mood to spend the night at Timberline."

"The lady feels tricked," Molly murmured as the manager walked away. Then she turned to Matt. "Just short of an avalanche, hmm?"

"What?"

"You said nothing short of an avalanche would keep us here."

"Clearly, I planned for the tree to fall."

She ignored that. "If we'd left earlier, when I was ready to go—"

"You didn't like the dessert?"

"That's not the point."

"Or maybe you didn't like the cappuccino?"

"It was delicious, but not necessary."

"And the dancing? Also delicious but not necessary?"

Matt backed up and headed down a bumpy, snow-covered side road.

"Where're you going?"

"To our executive chalet, Prescott, where else?"

8

MOLLY DIDN'T KNOW what to do or say. That surprised her. She should have known perfectly well how to handle the situation, and yet she'd never been in a situation quite like the one she was in now. Stranded on top of a mountain with Matt Kincaid.

Not stranded, actually. In fact, they were guests in a perfectly lovely chalet—A-frame with a high cathedral ceiling, rustic paneling, a huge stone fireplace and floor-to-ceiling windows. Any other time, Molly would have been charmed by the vacation home. But this wasn't a vacation, and this wasn't home. This was a problem.

As she walked around the chalet, commenting politely on the amenities Matt pointed out to her, she tried to calm down and convince herself there was nothing to get all worked up about. But she couldn't ignore that she was sharing the house with Matt. Logic told her that they had separate bedrooms, so the circumstances weren't really very different from those in Dillard.

Yet there was a difference. The house in Dillard was big, and they weren't alone in it. Krista's bedroom was just down the hall from Molly's. Here in the Timberline Chalet the bedrooms were right next to each other with no buffer zone.

Molly was going to have to do some scheming. She had never liked playing games, but tonight was special. If she didn't plan ahead, she could get into a lot of trouble. So she resolved to be cool and promised herself not to get into a long conversation with him, not to have a drink with him and certainly not to dance with him again. That had been her biggest mistake tonight. She'd just politely say good-night and go to bed.

"Which room do you want?" Matt asked after they finished their tour of the chalet.

"I—well, I'm not sure," Molly said. The larger bedroom was roomy and elegant with a double bed; the other was just as attractive, decorated in shades of rose and green, but had twin beds.

"I'll take the one with the double bed." As soon as Molly answered, she had a feeling he was laughing at her with his eyes. She didn't want him to start teasing; that could also lead them in the wrong direction.

"I guess I'm being bossy," she admitted. "Which bedroom would you like?"

"Doesn't matter to me. I can sleep anywhere." He wandered back into the living room. Logs were set up in the fireplace, and he took a long wooden match from a box on the mantelpiece, lit it and held it to the kindling. The flames leapt up immediately.

"We really don't need a fire," Molly told him. "It's quite warm, and I'm going to bed now anyway."

"Don't turn in yet. We need to call Krista," he added quickly.

"Yes, I guess we should."

"I'll call if you'll check out the bar. Rusty leaves a bottle for his guests, and a drink would suit me fine since I'm not going to be driving tonight."

Molly thought about her plan. She should be in her room now, door closed, in bed. But Matt was right; they needed to let Krista know what had happened so she wouldn't be worried.

"Krista? This is Matt." As he talked, Molly found a bottle of brandy and fixed his drink.

"Yes," he said into the phone, "we're still at the inn. Well, I decided to get Molly in a compromising situation."

Molly looked up, almost dropping the glass.

Matt was going strong. "I arranged the old we're-snowed-in-together-in-the-woods ploy, bribed a couple of guys to chop down a tree—"

"Matt!" Molly came out from behind the bar in an instant."

"I know, Kristabel," Matt continued. "It was a rotten thing to do, but—"

Molly made a lunge for the phone, but Matt sidestepped and went on talking. "I just couldn't resist her charms, and now that we're in this romantic setting I think she'll agree it was fate that brought us together, not a fallen tree."

On her next try, Molly managed to grab the phone. "Krista," she shouted into the receiver, "don't listen to him—" That was as far as she got when she heard the busy signal. She turned on Matt. "You—"

Trying not to laugh, Matt took the phone from her and hung it up.

"Your drink is on the bar. I'm going to bed."

"Wait, Molly."

That stopped her. "Why're you suddenly calling me by my first name?"

"I'm suddenly feeling very kindly toward you. I'm sorry about the joke with the phone. Sometimes I just can't resist teasing."

"Well, it wasn't funny," Molly said.

"I know." He stuck out his hand. "Truce?"

Molly nodded without shaking the offered hand.

"Now let me fix *you* a drink."

"No, thanks."

"Just one. Then we can try Krista again, and this time you do the explaining."

"I'll try her now."

"She's probably talking to Brent so it'll be a while."

"We'll see." Molly picked up the phone.

"If it's still busy will you have that drink?"

She nodded grudgingly and punched in the number. It was busy, and he'd already poured the brandy. There went her plan, Molly thought as she took the glass from him.

"Sorry for teasing you," Matt said gently.

"It's all right." Molly was very aware of his body next to hers. He'd taken off his coat and rolled up his sleeves. His arms were smooth and muscular; his hands strong and supple. Molly remembered how they'd danced—with his arms around her, he'd moved his hands along the contour of her neck. She felt herself blushing.

"If it's all right, why do you look so upset?"

"Upset?"

"Or something. You seem flushed." He raised his hand to her face, and rested his fingers lightly against her cheek.

"The fire . . ."

"Molly, the fire's across the room."

"Well, there's heat . . ."

He slid his hand to her neck. "I know. I feel it too."

Molly couldn't think of a response.

"That was a good idea I had, wasn't it?" With his thumb, he slowly and rhythmically caressed her jaw.

"What?" Her lips felt dry. She wet them with the tip of her tongue.

"Getting someone to cut down the tree."

"You didn't—"

"No—" Matt began to laugh "—I didn't."

Suddenly Molly was laughing, too, in spite of herself. Before she realized it, his arms were around her and she was laughing against his chest.

This wasn't in her plan at all. She moved away, attempting to smooth back her hair. "We have to call Krista."

"Later. She knows we can take care of ourselves."

"But you said—"

"That was then." He touched his finger lightly to her lips. "This is now."

"I don't—I can't—" Molly stammered senselessly.

"Molly, Molly." He ran his finger across her mouth.

Acting totally on instinct, she parted her lips, tasting the salty warmth of his fingers.

"Don't you know what you do to me, Molly?"

She didn't know, couldn't tell how he felt. She only knew how she felt—as if she were melting. To stop what was happening between them, she needed to act now. He was going to kiss her.

He leaned forward. Molly turned away, but Matt put his lips next to her ear. His breath stirred the tendrils of her hair, caressed her neck and tickled the tender flesh of her earlobe.

"I just want to kiss you, Molly." He whispered. "We've kissed before."

"But we don't—we don't get along," she said feebly. "We fight and argue and . . ."

He kissed her neck, sending goose bumps up and down her backbone.

"We challenge each other, Molly. That's what you mean. We both love challenges."

As he talked softly to her, Matt pulled the pins from her hair; she felt it cascade to her shoulders. He held her head with one hand so that she had to meet his eyes. "You're not afraid of challenges, are you, Molly? Or of me?"

"I'm scared to death, Matt Kincaid," she murmured.

"But you want to kiss me, don't you?"

Molly reached up and touched his lips with her fingertips. He stood silently as she moved her trembling fingers across his mouth and then took them away.

"Molly—"

She stood on tiptoe and placed her lips where her fingers had been. Their kiss was just as she remembered, warm and demanding. She opened her mouth under his and drew his tongue inside, tasting him and letting him taste her. Her breasts were crushed against the fabric of his shirt. Her nipples were taut and tight, and sensations of pleasure exploded inside her as he held her close. She felt the kiss from the tips of her toes to the top of her head.

He didn't stop but kept on kissing her, nibbling on her lower lip, exploring with his tongue, letting his lips drift to her neck and cheek before discovering her mouth again. She could feel the heat of his body and the tenseness of his muscles; she could feel his strength and his desire.

He stopped long enough to toss the pillows off the sofa. "Now there's room," he whispered softly as he lowered her onto the sofa. "It's as good as a bed." He lay down beside her, half covering her with the length of his body.

"This is crazy," she managed.

"It's the least crazy thing we've ever done, Molly." He began kissing the sensitive skin beneath her chin and along her neck. Molly almost purred with satisfaction.

"You're still calling me Molly," she murmured.

"Prescott is the editor I argue with. Molly is the woman I want to make love to . . . more than anything. Are we going to make love, Molly?"

"Ever since we first came in."

"What?" he asked.

"You've been calling me Molly ever since we came into the chalet."

"Yes, I've wanted to make love to you since then." He laughed softly. "To tell the truth, I've wanted that from the start—even when I was calling you Prescott. You've wanted it too, Molly."

Molly didn't tell him how long. She wasn't sure herself because she'd tried to ignore the feelings. But she hadn't been able to ignore them since they came into the chalet. She'd known what would happen and that's why she'd formulated her plan, but her plan had now been abandoned. She'd meant to be strong and determined; instead she was hot and bothered, nervous and happy all at the same time.

As a response to his words, she took his hand and placed it on her breast. She heard his intake of breath. He was still for a moment and then began to stroke her tender nipple through the soft fabric.

"I'd like to taste you, too. Here." He rubbed the taut bud with his fingertip. "And here." He moved his other hand between her legs, caressing her gently.

Molly's heart was racing frantically. The warmth of his hands caused sensations of pleasure to wash over her.

She slipped her hand between their bodies to feel the hardness of his erection. She closed her eyes and stroked him through the rough fabric of his jeans.

"Oh, Molly," he groaned, his breath coming fast and harsh. "This is torture, but wonderful torture." He kissed her, running his tongue along her teeth, touching the roof of her mouth, sucking on her tongue. "I want to undress you and see you in the firelight. I want to kiss you and . . ."

His words faded away. Or maybe he was still talking to her, making love to her with his voice, but she seemed to be in a dream. Then she felt his hands at the buttons of her blouse, at the clasp of her bra. His mouth, hot and seeking, was on her breast. Pleasure radiated throughout her body, and deep inside she felt a tightening of her muscles, a throbbing that made her writhe beneath him.

The chalet was dark, but from across the room the light from the flickering fire danced on the ceiling and reflected on their bodies as they undressed each other.

"I want to look at you," he whispered. "So lovely, so delicate." With his fingers, Matt traced the line of her rib cage, the indentation of her waist. "My sweet Molly. You're so beautiful."

"And you, too," she said softly. "Just beautiful." She touched him, exploring the width of his chest, the tight muscles of his back, and finally his erection. She touched him with her fingers, caressed him, then held him gently but firmly, moving her hand up and down.

"You please me so much, Molly. I want to do the same for you, to touch you, kiss you, taste you all over. I want this night to last and last...."

Molly closed her eyes. "So do I, Matt. So do I."

He traced a path with his mouth from her breast to her hipbone, pausing to nibble, before he reached the softness between her legs. Molly shifted so that his mouth and tongue could please her. But it was more than pleasure that he gave her; it was passion, hot, sweet passion flooding through her. Her skin flamed with desire and her veins pulsed with excitement.

Her cries of ecstasy slowly changed to moans of need. "I want you, Matt," she whispered. "I want you inside of me."

In his fantasies he'd made love to Molly again and again, but this was better than any dream. To hold her, to kiss her and feel her lithe, sweet body against his. Her touch, her kiss, even the look of passion in her eyes moved him. The firelight flickered on the creaminess of her skin, making her body glow. Her dark hair shone like ebony.

"I want to be there more than anything."

She held his arousal in her hands, guided him to her soft and yielding moistness. Gently, fighting for control, he slid into her warmth.

Matt moved slowly at first, not wanting to break the magic web that held them. Molly responded at the same pace, moving with him, lifting her hips toward his. Her eyes were closed, her head flung back. The look on her face was one of such abandon that Matt felt as though he would explode. He didn't want it ever to end. Not ever.

But he couldn't hold back, nor could she. Together they moved faster and faster, their bodies slippery and damp. He heard Molly laugh with joy, and he felt the same happiness as they moved, their sensations spiraling, their passion fueling each other's fire.

When their release came it was powerful. They clung to each other, kissing damply until at last they were calm, moving more and more slowly. Then not at all. Still, they held each other tightly, his arms wrapped securely around her, her head nestled comfortably against his shoulder.

Matt kissed her eyelids, her nose, the corner of her mouth. "Who said nothing in life was perfect? That, my dear Molly, was perfection."

She looked up at him shyly through lowered lids. "It was wonderful . . . you were wonderful." She touched his face. "So sweet and loving and—" She stopped herself.

"And? Keep on, Molly. Keep on."

"And so sexy." She hid her face again, burying it against his shoulder. "Oh, Matt! What we did together."

"That's only a taste of what we'll be doing . . ." Matt stood up, put his arms around her and lifted her off the sofa ". . . once we get into bed."

"Which bed?" she said shyly.

He strode across the room with Molly in his arms. "Your big double bed, Molly. With plenty of room for both of us."

THEY MADE LOVE AGAIN, this time more slowly. They watched each other's faces as their pleasure flowed and ebbed, then built to a torrent of passion. Molly couldn't get enough of Matt, of his kisses, the feeling of his body against hers, the way his muscles ran in smooth ridges across his back, the way he felt when he was deep inside of her.

"Carried away . . ." she murmured at last against his mouth. "Carried away. . . . I know what that means now."

"You're not the only one."

She ran her fingers along his face and touched the scar she'd noticed before. "What happened?"

"I could tell you a story about climbing Everest and rescuing a stranded climber or about fighting off the Yeti in the Himalayas or—"

Molly kissed the scar. "The truth, Matt."

"The truth?"

"Mmm."

"I fell off the porch roof—"

Molly laughed.

"—when I was a teenager."

"What were you doing up there?"

"Sneaking into my room very late one night after a hot date with a girl across town. I was wildly in love."

Molly put her fingers to his lips. "That's a story I don't want to hear. Not now, not tonight. Tonight, I want you all to myself."

Matt pulled her on top of him, moving his hands down her body and cupping her bottom lovingly. "You have me, Molly. All night long."

LATER, THEY REMEMBERED to call Krista and then sometime in the middle of the night they showered together. Bathing each other, they explored the wonder of their new intimacy.

"This can't be happening to me," Molly whispered as Matt slowly dried her with a big fluffy towel. "You and me . . . the shower . . ."

"Not to mention the sofa and the bed." He rubbed the towel over her thighs. "Just enjoy the moment, Molly. I certainly am."

Enjoy the moment. She shut her eyes and let the pleasure of Matt's touch wash over her like the warm water that had just cleansed them. But what about tomorrow? she thought. What about tomorrow?

MOLLY WIGGLED AND TRIED to move. Her hair was caught under Matt's shoulder. One of his legs was hooked over hers. His arm pinned her around the waist. The phone was ringing, but Matt only moaned without budging.

Molly had to lift his arm, squeeze out from under his leg, and shift her body so that she could grab the phone.

"Road's clear," a voice announced.

"Rusty, good morning," Molly said.

"You can move out anytime."

"Thanks," she said, "and thanks for the chalet."

"My pleasure. Come back again. And stay until ten this morning if you'd like. After that we need to get the chalet ready for our next guests."

"No problem, Rusty." She hung up and sank back onto the pillow, snuggling next to Matt.

He was awake, watching her out of drowsy eyes. "Road clear?"

"Yep. And Rusty reminds us we have to leave by ten."

Matt pulled her close, and she basked in the warmth that emanated from his body. "Sun's just up. We have plenty of time." He tightened his embrace. "Who said we couldn't be on the same side, Prescott? We're certainly on the same side now, at least the same side of the bed. We slept cuddled up like spoons last night."

Molly had tensed when he said her name. Prescott. Was she Prescott again? Matt seemed not to have noticed.

"I guess we ought to start back," she said tentatively.

Matt didn't answer immediately. He stroked her arm pensively. "I was thinking. Why do we have to go back at all?"

Molly turned to look at him. "Well, for lots of reasons. The caterer. The baker. Pete. Who's probably running around doing who knows what. And then there's the small matter of the wedding."

"Oh, that." Matt chuckled.

"Yes, that."

"But think of all the other possibilities. We could hang out here. . . ."

"They're booked up, remember?"

He kissed her neck familiarly, and she felt herself relax into his arms, remembering the night before, remembering their closeness.

"Then what about just taking off?" he asked, nuzzling lovingly. "We could drive to Denver, get tickets to—what would be fun? Where have you always wanted to go? Hawaii, Fiji? I hear Bali is great."

"I've always had the urge to see Tahiti. . . ."

"Sounds great."

"I know. I've done a lot of reading about the island— Hey, wait a minute!" Molly turned over and leaned up on one elbow. "I'm not going anywhere except Dillard."

Matt was still lying back, eyes closed. He lifted one eyebrow casually at her words.

"Are you serious about this?" Molly asked.

He opened his eyes wide. "Of course, I'm serious. Tahiti would be great. They go topless there, don't they? That would be nice, to see you topless on the beach." Matt's hand sneaked under the cover and found her breast.

Molly pulled away. "We can't go to Tahiti or anywhere else. I'm working. Your sister is counting on me. I can't go running off with you on some kind of island adventure."

"Sure you can, Prescott."

There it was again, and this time she decided to call him on it. "So I'm Prescott now? That must mean we're arguing."

"You're arguing. I'm offering an opportunity."

"No, thanks, *Kincaid*." She started to get out of bed, but Matt grabbed her around the waist and pulled her against him.

"Just listen to me." He nuzzled the back of her neck. "You and I take off for Tahiti. Just for a few days, but if we decide to stay longer..."

"Brent and Krista are getting married in four days."

"They can postpone it for a while. No harm done." He snuggled against her back and kissed her on the shoulder. "It'll give them a chance to rethink things."

At that Molly pulled away from him and stood up. She'd forgotten that she was nude until she saw the glimmer of desire in Matt's eyes as he looked her up and down. She grabbed a quilt from the foot of the bed and wrapped herself in it. Now fully covered and standing on her feet, she felt a little more in control. "Is that what you had in mind? Did you think that after spending one night—"

"We didn't spend the night, we made love," Matt corrected.

"Whatever," Molly snapped. "But after one night, did you think I was going to forget my job, the story, or Brent and Krista and run off with you to Tahiti? They're counting on me. You must be crazy, Kincaid."

Matt, seemingly oblivious to the fact that he was also nude, swung his feet over the side of the bed and onto the floor. "I'm not crazy, Prescott. Think about it. There's definitely something between us. You felt it last night just as much as I did. It was unbelievable. And if you're bothered because it was just one night, then go away with me, and we can make love tonight, tomorrow, indefinitely."

"You're missing the point, as usual." Molly dragged the trailing quilt behind her and looked into the mirror above the dresser. Her hair tumbled wildly around her face, her cheeks were flushed and there were marks on her neck from Matt's love nibbles.

"Oh, Lord," she cried. "I look like hell."

"I think you look great. Come back to bed. We have plenty of time."

Molly turned to look at him. "You don't understand, do you, Kincaid? I'm not coming back to bed. I'm not running away with you to Tahiti. I'm not under any circumstances giving up plans for the wedding. And if this seduction was for that purpose—"

"I didn't seduce you, Prescott, and you know it."

Memories of the night suffused her and her head began to swim. She shook away the feeling. "Yes, I do know it. And it was a big mistake."

"Why? Because we enjoyed ourselves? Isn't that allowed?"

"No! I mean yes!" she shouted. "We're allowed to enjoy ourselves, but you're trying to use our night together to lead me away from Dillard. Well, it's not working. You can't manipulate me that easily, Matt Kincaid. And frankly I can't believe you'd be so low and calculating."

She stumbled toward the door, catching her heel in the trailing quilt. "I'm going to find my clothes and put them on, and then we're going back to Dillard so I can get on with the wedding."

She exited with as much dignity as she could muster under the circumstances.

Matt remained on the bed, thinking. He'd been serious about the trip. He couldn't imagine anything more fun—or more exciting—than to take off for a while with Molly. At first he hadn't even considered the effect that would have on the wedding, but now she was twisting it around to make it seem like that had been his purpose.

He heard her in the next room cursing softly as she dressed. Matt paused thoughtfully for a moment, then went to the door. Molly looked up from buttoning her blouse. He could see the anger flashing in her eyes.

"Prescott," he said softly, "you may not believe me, but there was nothing calculated about last night. It was spontaneous and perfect."

He saw her eyes waver for a moment and her face soften. Then she tightened her jaw and lifted her chin in a gesture he'd come to know so well.

"It doesn't matter now."

"Yes, it does. It's important to me that you understand. My asking you to go away had nothing to do with Krista and Brent."

"Oh, no? It just happened to come right after we'd made love and right before the wedding. That's not calculated?"

"It wasn't meant to be."

"Just coincidence, Kincaid?"

Matt smiled. "Well, I must admit postponing the wedding would be a nice plus. But a secondary one," he added quickly.

She bent down and picked up his clothes. "I'm tired of your teasing, Matt. This isn't the time or the place for it. So put your pants on. The sun's up and it's a new day."

Matt managed to catch the clothes she threw at him before they came hurtling into his face.

AN HOUR LATER they pulled into the Kincaid driveway. A Jeep was blocking their way. Molly gave a groan. She wasn't ready to face Pete so early.

Matt opened his door. "This is where you wanted to be, Prescott. Back in Dillard."

"Yep, I know." Wearily, she climbed out. He'd attempted to placate her on the drive, but she'd refused his overtures. What more was there to say? She'd given herself wholly and totally to Matt, only to find that he wanted a deal—a few hot nights in Tahiti for the cancellation of Krista's wedding. No matter how much Matt denied it, he was trying to buy her off. To her shame, she'd almost fallen for it.

Silently they walked into the house. Pete was at the kitchen counter. "Hi. Saw you pull up. Thought you might want coffee." He held out two mugs.

Matt took one. "I'm going upstairs to shave and change. Where's Krista?" he asked brusquely.

"Went over to the store. Said she had to open up."

Matt nodded and left the room. Molly took the other cup of coffee and gulped half of it down. It was rich and strong. "What are you doing here?" she asked Pete.

"Well, good morning to you, too, Miss Sunshine."

"Sorry to be grouchy, but why are you here, Pete? Did you do as I asked and take the photos of Dillard?"

"One question at a time, Molly. I'll answer the second one first. I took the pictures yesterday. Then I came over last night to see you and learned you and the King of the Mountain had gone out to dinner. So I waited around. When you didn't come home...." He raised an eyebrow.

"You didn't spend the night here, did you, Pete?"

"Nope. But I stayed for a long time. It was pretty late when Matt called."

Molly didn't respond to his comment.

"I was very chaste and circumspect, Molly. Now, to answer your next question, I came over today on the assumption that you'd finally be back. Where did you and Kincaid spend the night, anyway? At the inn?"

Molly went to the counter and poured another cup of coffee. She didn't want Pete to see her face. "There was a tree across the road—"

"I know that, Molly."

"Well, we stayed at one of the chalets. A two-bedroom one." She turned to face him, defiantly daring him to say more.

"Okay, fine, babe. No problem. You're a big girl." He seemed, at least for the moment, to lose interest in her and Matt. "The proof sheets of my photos will be ready in an hour. You'll like 'em. Nice shots of Dillard, the old houses, the shops, Kincaid, Limited. And with my filters and great angles, there won't be a flake of snow in sight. You'll swear it's June in Colorado. So what's on tap for today?"

"The caterer. I want you with me to explain the food look we need. Damn, I wish we had a food stylist for the lobster."

"We'll work it out, babe. You look bushed, though. Are you sure you don't want to crash for a while?"

"I slept fine last night," Molly lied. "I'll just change clothes and get myself together. And then we need to have a little talk."

"About the shoot?"

"No, not about the shoot. About how you aren't going to argue with Brent anymore and how you aren't going to be alone with Krista. At all. Ever. I know your reputation, Pete."

He looked at her, a big grin on his face. "If you'd been here last night, we would have had a chaperone. But you were in the mountains."

"Last night was beyond my control," Molly said as she stalked into the hallway. "In more ways than one."

9

IN THE FRONT HALL of the Kincaid home, Molly watched Pete Walenski do what he did best—take pictures. The subject was the bride-to-be modeling her wedding dress.

Pete was being very talkative. "Perfect. That's it, Krista, take a breath. Hold it. Wet your lips. Now smile. Turn your head. You're getting into the mood, enjoying yourself. Laugh. Louder, louder! You're gorgeous, just gorgeous."

Pete circled Krista with the camera to his eye, talking and snapping without pause. That was his style, and it was necessary for him to achieve perfect pictures. Molly had seen it often. As she observed him working she kept telling herself this wasn't unusual.

But did he have to keep reminding Krista of how beautiful she was? As Molly watched, she tried to remain outwardly calm and professional, even though she was churning inside.

Light bounced off photo umbrellas and the camera whirred as Pete shuffled across a floor cluttered with Polaroid shots that had been used for testing and had been discarded.

"She's a natural, Molly. This session is going to be historic."

Molly nodded. "No doubt about it." The feeling of unease wouldn't go away. It had gripped her every time Krista and Pete came near each other, and this shoot was no exception.

But of course it was necessary. She certainly couldn't do without photos of the bride in her wedding gown. Mentally, she kept reassuring herself that everything was going well. In spite of his effusion, Pete was being completely professional. As for Krista, she was being herself: friendly, cooperative, charming, but no more so than usual. And Pete was right—she was drop-dead gorgeous in her Victorian wedding gown.

Molly was having trouble deciding whether or not the young people were flirting. If anyone else had been watching, they'd almost certainly deny it. On the surface, there seemed only to be friendliness on Pete's part, and respect on Krista's. Nothing else showed. Even Molly couldn't see it. But she felt it. There was something more going on between them.

If she could catch Pete actually flirting, then she'd have an excuse to stop the shoot, stop everything, even send Pete away and get someone else flown in. If not, she'd have to hang in there and hope it was all her imagination. She couldn't fire him from the job for no reason.

She willed herself to get through the shoot and the next three days. Then she'd be able to say goodbye to the Kincaids forever. Until then, she couldn't help feeling jumpy and on edge.

Matt wasn't helping at all. She kept trying to avoid him, but he seemed to be everywhere, watching her in his bemused and slightly cynical way. He obviously wanted to talk about what had gone on between them at Timberline. She didn't.

Why was she staying away from him? Molly told herself she was embarrassed to have let her emotions get out of hand, to have gotten involved with a member of the bride's family. There was probably some kind of *Wedding* magazine rule against that.

But it wasn't the real reason. The truth was, Molly was confused. But not just confused. It was much more than that. She was a mass of emotions. Scared. Embarrassed. Tense. Not to mention insecure, wondering if she'd been just another in a long list of women Matt had taken to bed.

She shook those thoughts out of her head and forced her attention on the problem at hand. "Aren't you almost finished, Pete?" She asked the question more sharply than she meant to; she'd been doing that a lot lately.

"Almost. I just need a few more. Close-ups, I think. We haven't concentrated on Krista's face yet. And it's a face of incredible—"

"Just shoot, Pete. Don't talk. We have a tight schedule. There's the shower this afternoon and the party tonight—"

She was interrupted by someone knocking at the back door.

"It's probably Brent's mom with the flowers," Krista said.

"Quiet," Pete advised her. "I want your mouth completely relaxed."

Krista complied.

"Perfect. Just what I wanted."

"I'll get the door." Molly was a little nervous about leaving the two young people alone, so she hurried into the kitchen, prepared to haul Suzanne back with her.

It wasn't Suzanne; it was Brent.

"Is Krista here?"

"Yes, she is."

"Great."

"But you can't see her."

Brent frowned. "Whatta you mean? I need to talk to her."

"No, Brent—"

"Look, Molly, I don't want to seem pushy, but Krista *is* my fiancée, we *are* getting married in three days, so I'm afraid no one—even you—is going to tell me I can't see her."

"Brent, I'm sorry, but she's having her picture taken—"

Brent headed toward the front of the house. "Where, in here?"

Molly reached for him. "She's in her wedding dress." She latched onto his jacket.

"What is this, Molly?"

"Don't you know? It's one of the cardinal wedding rules. The groom can't see his bride in her gown until the wedding."

"That's ridiculous."

"No, it's not, and you're well aware of it. Krista would be really upset if you went in there."

Just then there was a burst of laughter from the hall-way.

"He's with her, right?"

"If by 'he,' you mean Pete, of course. He's the photographer."

"I don't like them alone. In fact, I don't like him near her at all."

"They aren't alone," Molly assured him. "I mean, they weren't alone. I was with them, and I'm going right back. You can see Krista tonight."

"What about this afternoon?"

"That'll be girl time. The shower, remember? I was actually expecting your mom with the decorations."

"Is that another wedding rule—no men at the shower?"

"A big-time rule."

"Will *he* be there?"

Molly flinched at his use of the word "he" because it revealed the depth of Brent's frustration. "Pete will be taking pictures at the shower, but they won't exactly be alone. Your mom—"

"I know. The bridesmaids—"

"Krista's girlfriends—"

"And the photographer."

"He's necessary, Brent."

"And I'm not."

Molly shook her head, laughing. "I guess we'd have to say you're not, at least not this afternoon. But in three days you'll be the only one who matters."

"Three days or an eternity. Whichever comes first. Meanwhile, I'm a fifth wheel."

Molly pulled him back toward the door. "Weddings can be a tough time for the groom. It'll all be worth it when you see Krista coming down that staircase."

Brent shrugged. "Okay, Molly. I'll see you tonight at the real party."

"Oh, yes. It's at the Bugaloo Club...."

Now Brent laughed as he paused at the door, his good nature returning. "The Buckaroo, Molly. Get the idea? It's country-western, casual wear. Put on your cowboy boots."

"For dancing?"

"Sure. The kind of dancing we'll be doing calls for cowboy boots. We do some real stomping out there."

"Well, I'll give it a try. See you tonight."

Molly waited until Brent was out the door and it had closed behind him before she sprinted through the kitchen and out to the hallway.

Krista had gone, and Pete was loading up his equipment.

"Great shoot, babe. Your picture editor is going to have a hell of a time choosing from these proofs."

"That's good."

Pete looked up, frowning.

"I mean, great."

"You seem distracted. Trouble in the kitchen?"

"Not really. I was expecting Suzanne, but it was Brent, looking for Krista. Of course, he can't see her in the dress, and he can't come to the shower, so he's a little irritated. But there's a party tonight. He can claim his bride at that."

"And will, I'm sure. How about you?"

"What are you talking about?"

"Who's claiming you tonight? Are you hooked up with the mountain man?"

"Hardly," Molly said dryly.

"Then we'll go together. Sure he won't object?"

"He won't object."

Pete packed the lights into canvas bags and stacked them in the corner. "Lover's tiff?" he teased.

"Don't be ridiculous." Molly started up the stairs.

"Wait a minute, babe." Pete grabbed her hand and pulled her down to sit on the wide stairway beside him. "Let's talk."

Molly saw the spark of interest in Pete's eyes and knew he wasn't going to let up until he found out a few things. She was relieved in a way because she needed someone to talk to. Pete was available and, despite her recent concerns about him, he had proved in the past to be a good friend and a good listener.

"*Did* you have a tiff?"

"It wasn't that at all." Molly took a deep breath. "Matt asked me to go to Tahiti with him—"

"Great."

"No, Pete, it's not."

"Tahiti? It's supposed to be fabulous. It's one of the spots I haven't visited but always wanted to."

"Then maybe you can go with Matt."

"Somehow I don't think it would be the same," Pete said with a grin. "So why don't you go? After the wedding's over, you'll need some R and R."

"After the wedding, I have to get back to New York to edit the story, work on the layout—in short, do my job. Besides, the invitation wasn't for after the wedding. It was for now, immediately."

"Oh," Pete said slowly. "Now or never?"

"That's the feeling I got. Of course, he's saying that he didn't mean that at all, that we can go anytime."

"But you think it was a setup to get you out of here?"

"That's the idea."

He looked at her sideways. "You didn't by any chance jump to conclusions, did you, Molly? You have a habit of doing that."

"Whether I did or not, the invitation came at a very opportune time."

"After a night of passionate love—"

Molly moved away to show her irritation. "I didn't say that."

"You didn't have to."

"Pete, I really don't want to talk about this." Molly made an attempt to get up.

Pete grasped her arm. "Let me just finish my thought. After a night of love, Matt asks you to go away with him for presumably more of the same. You see that as a bribe to forget the wedding which, as we all know, he's been wanting to do all along."

"That's about it," Molly confirmed glumly as he released her arm.

"What if he really didn't have that in mind?"

"Pete, it doesn't matter because I'm not going."

"Not now. What about later?"

"That wouldn't work. I told you, I have to go back to New York. It's pretty likely that I won't ever see Matt Kincaid again."

"I'm beginning to see the light," Pete said, jumping up to make his point. "You want to go away with this guy, but you want it on your terms. After the wedding, after the editing, when it's convenient." He leaned close. "Well, Molly, my dear, take it from an old-timer, love isn't always convenient. Sometimes it hits you when you least expect it. It could very well have hit Matt last night, making him react by asking you away with him, forgetting for the moment all about the wedding. That's what love does. Love, the ol' devil, isn't a very good planner."

Molly sat up alertly and looked sharply at Pete. "Are you trying to tell me something about what's happened to you?"

"Don't change the subject. I'm trying to tell you something about yourself, Moll. I think you're falling for this guy. I think you'd love to run off to Tahiti with him, but just because he asked you at the wrong time, you're backing off. I think my strong, brave Molly Prescott might just be afraid of getting involved, so she's making her lover into an opportunist. Which he's not and you know it."

"I don't know any such thing, and neither do you. Matt Kincaid is not only the most high-handed and manipulative—"

"He's also making the rules, and that drives you crazy because you like to be in charge."

Pete flopped back down on the stairs at the same moment that Molly stood up. "I've had enough of this talk about love. No one is in love around here but Brent and Krista."

"Pardon me, boss, but they may just be the only two who're *not*."

"What in the world does that mean?"

"Think about it."

"Not even for a minute," Molly said resolutely. "They're in love, they're getting married in three days and I don't want to hear anything else about it. Now I'm going up to change for the bridal shower." Molly headed up the stairs with Pete right behind her.

"You have to watch out for love, babe. It's like . . . what's it like?"

"Don't ask me. It's your subject."

"A pit bull?"

"What!" Molly laughed.

"No, too big. A snake?"

"Sounds about right," Molly said, still laughing.

"No. Too vicious. I've got it. Love's like a bee. It'll sting you when you least expect it."

"This conversation is over, Pete."

Pete suddenly became serious and, when they arrived at Molly's room, he reached out to touch her shoulder. "I know what it's like, Molly. It's scary as hell to fall in love, especially at the wrong time. But if it's the right person, you don't need to be afraid."

"I'm not afraid." Molly opened the door and stepped into her room. "And if you don't quit talking about it, you won't have a date for the party tonight."

Safely in her room, Molly tried to ignore the sound of Pete's laughter fading down the hall. But there was one thing she couldn't ignore: Pete was right. She *was* afraid, afraid of her feelings for Matt, afraid she might fall for him even harder than she already had. But most of all, Molly was afraid she'd be hurt. She needed to protect herself, and the only way to do that was to avoid him as much as possible until after the wedding. And then get out of there.

Three more days until the wedding and counting, Molly told herself. If she could just make it until blast-off.

THE KINCAID PARLOR WAS a mess. Discarded gift wrap covered the floor. Diane rummaged among the colorful paper, collecting the used ribbons, to fashion a corsage for Krista to carry at the wedding rehearsal. Lisa was trying to keep a list of gifts but kept getting sidetracked.

"Who gave you the blue nightgown?" she called out to Krista.

"That was two gifts ago, Lisa," someone else said. "Let Suzanne keep the list."

Suzanne, pouring some kind of unusual punch she'd made—from all-natural ingredients, Molly imagined—declined adamantly. "Lists aren't my thing. I can't even handle a grocery list."

Krista's girlfriends had outdone themselves in their choice of gifts for the lingerie shower. Suzanne's was the most exotic, which didn't surprise Molly in the least. It was a handmade silk robe in sunset colors of rose and peach and lavender decorated with panels of lace.

Some of the other guests weren't so prudish in their choices; Krista had received a good supply of filmy gowns, lacy camisoles and sexy bikini undies. The opening of each gift brought on giggles and shrieks of delight, all enjoyed by the only man in the room, Pete Walenski.

When he wasn't busy shifting lights, readjusting settings, standing on a chair or lying on the floor to get his shots, Pete watched from the sidelines, a thoughtful look on his face. After a series of wide-angle shots of the whole party, he began to center in on Krista. Soon she became the focus of every picture.

Finally Molly pulled on his sleeve, leaned over and whispered, "Get some of the buffet table."

"I already did, Molly. You weren't watching. Now the table looks like the Mongol hordes have been through it. Totally wasted. You want shots of leftover food?"

"Well, no, but I could use some of the bridesmaids. They're all lovely."

"Yeah, yeah. Lovely." He turned the lens on Krista. "I'll get them for you, but not now. I like this series of Krista."

Molly gave up and, feeling anything but festive, tried to enjoy the rest of the festivities.

Unfortunately Krista seemed anything but jubilant herself as she opened her presents. Holding up each item for everyone to see, she thanked each gift giver effusively. But something was missing. There should have been some kind of excitement in the air as the bride-to-be contemplated all the glamorous lingerie she'd be showing off to her new husband. It was missing.

Alison, an outgoing redhead, tried to liven up the proceedings with sexy little insinuations, but Krista just didn't respond.

Alison gave a long low whistle when Krista pulled the next present out of its wrappings—a lacy black nightgown. "Now this is something that's going to be a total waste."

"A waste? I think it's gorgeous." Krista smiled her thanks.

"But how long is Brent going to let you keep it on? About two seconds, I'll bet, and that gown will be a heap on the floor."

Krista laughed with the others, but her good humor seemed forced. Molly snatched a look at Pete. He seemed stricken, and when his eyes met Krista's, Molly swore she saw despair in both of their faces.

It was time, she knew, for another long talk with Pete. She'd had a chance earlier but he'd sidetracked her into talking about her feelings toward Matt instead of about Pete's feelings toward Krista. Molly wanted to believe that Krista's stress was due to wedding jitters and nothing more. But it was getting difficult.

"There's one more present," Lisa called out. "And look who it's for." She paused dramatically. "Molly Prescott."

Molly snapped out of her reverie. "For me?"

"Yes!" Krista clapped her hands and seemed animated for the first time. "It's a thank-you present for everything you've done for me. I thought it would be fun for you to have a present, too."

Molly was thrilled and touched. Excitedly she tore off the ribbon and paper. She lifted the lid of the box and pulled out a shimmer of red lace and satin. "Oh, my gosh . . ."

"Isn't it fabulous?" Krista seemed more excited about Molly's present than any of her own. "It's a teddy. Hold it up."

Molly complied so that everyone could see the one-piece satin teddy with its lace insets placed at strategic points. It would be the sexiest thing by far in Molly's wardrobe. "It's wonderful. Almost too sexy to wear."

"Don't say that, Molly. You're wearing it tonight to the party—"

There was a burst of laughter at that, and Suzanne called out, "Under jeans and a shirt, I hope. It's a family affair."

"Pete, could you get a shot? I want a picture of Molly and her teddy," Krista requested.

For the first time there seemed to be a sense of spontaneity and joy among the guests.

"Move, everyone, so you don't block the shot." Krista called out. "This'll be great. I'll put it in my scrapbook...."

"Stand up, Moll," Pete ordered. "Let's get the full view. Or how about making a quick change and modeling it."

"In your dreams," Molly countered, but she stood up and held the teddy draped over her body, posing provocatively. She felt like a fool, but her audience seemed happy and, after all, this was a party. It was supposed to be fun, and if she could contribute to the good mood, she certainly would.

She was so wrapped up in the moment that she didn't hear him come in. But she heard the exclamations.

"No men allowed!"

"Don't peek, Matt!"

Then she heard his voice. "Just passing through, ladies. Looks like you're having quite a party."

The female chatter continued as Molly looked up and her eyes met his. He was standing in the doorway and there was a shine of mist on his hair from the light rain that was falling outside. He looked very out of place among the women in their bright dresses—a masculine presence in a swirl of femininity.

Alison offered him a glass of wine, Krista showed him some of her presents and Suzanne shoved a plate of shrimp at him. All the while, Matt looked over their heads at Molly. She was still sitting there with the fiery red teddy pressed against her blouse. Was it her imagination or could she feel its heat permeate her silk shirt?

She couldn't take her eyes off his face. His lips curved in a smile, and there was hunger in his eyes. Excitement sparked between them. It was as if they were the only two people in the room.

She dropped her eyes and looked away. Matt turned his attention to the other women, and the moment passed. But Molly felt its effect long afterward.

He gestured to her a little later, and something urged her to follow him into the hall.

"I need to add my approval of that little red thing you were holding up," he told her.

"A gift from your sister."

"And a very good choice." Matt leaned close, his breath warm on her cheek. "Just the thought of you in it, Molly—those little patches of lace—you can't imagine what that does to me."

Molly took a shaky breath and backed away half a step. The wall stopped her retreat. Instinctively she crossed her arms snugly over her abdomen as if for protection, but her gesture was futile. She could feel Matt undressing her with his eyes.

Slowly he reached out to touch her cheek with his fingertips. The sounds of the party echoed around her, but faintly, as if from a great distance.

"Remember to pack that red thing for our trip," he whispered.

"Our trip?" she repeated foolishly.

"To Tahiti." He trailed his fingers lightly across her lips, letting them linger there. Then he grinned at her, turned, and walked up the stairs.

Molly leaned against the wall, her heart pounding wildly. She touched her lips where Matt's fingertips had been. How, with just a touch, did he manage to turn her world upside down?

"Molly!" someone called from the parlor.

She took a deep breath, stood up straight—without the support of the wall—and forced herself to go back into the women-filled room.

AFTER THE PARTY was over, and she'd helped clean up, Molly hugged Krista warmly and then went up to her room. Feeling strangely disconnected from herself, as if she were an actress in a play, she showered, washed her hair and toweled it dry. It fell to her shoulders in restless waves. For a change she didn't bother to pin it up, but left it loose and curling.

She smoothed her body with lotion and applied her makeup carefully. Then she stepped into her new teddy and stood back to look at her reflection in the mirror.

Krista had guessed the size exactly. The satin clung to her like a glove and the lace cupped her breasts snugly. As she fastened the tiny covered buttons, her hands trembled. In fact, she felt shaky all over, burning with an inner excitement she didn't try to contain. She thought of the hunger she'd seen in Matt's eyes.

Molly pulled on her jeans and turtleneck sweater over the teddy. The feel of lace and satin against her skin was sensual, like the caress of a warm hand.

She looked at herself in the mirror one more time and fluffed out her hair. Then she went downstairs to meet her date for the party. But Pete Walenski wasn't the man in her thoughts or in her heart.

10

THE BUCKAROO CLUB WAS noisy and smoky, and the local country-and-western band was playing too loudly for Matt's taste. It was definitely not his style, but Krista's friends seemed to be having a great time.

Their table was laden with half-empty glasses of soft drinks, long-necked beer bottles and trays of nachos and barbecued chicken wings. The young people laughed and joked with one another above the music.

Alison was on one side of Matt, Diane on the other, and both of them tried to draw him into flirtatious conversation. He felt as though he were being crushed by adoring employees. He also felt uncomfortable but, for Krista's sake, he tried to be pleasant. But he kept wondering what the hell was keeping Molly. She would come, he had no doubt about that. Molly wouldn't miss another photo opportunity for *Wedding*. But where was she?

Alison jabbered on, gesturing with her hands as she talked. Matt nodded occasionally but didn't pay any attention to what she was saying. He'd tuned her out, and instead he watched the door, waiting. Every time it swung open, he grew tense and alert.

Five minutes passed without any movement at the doorway, then it opened again. His heart quickened when he saw Molly and Pete walk in. At the same time he felt a sudden unexpected burst of jealousy. They looked good together, comfortable, friendly. He watched closely as they sat down at the far end of the table. Molly seemed consciously to avoid meeting his eyes.

"Matt. *Matt*," Alison repeated. "I've asked you to dance twice. Is there some kind of rule that a boss can't dance with his employee?"

"Absolutely not," Matt answered without enthusiasm. Then, abashed by his insensitivity, he added, "Besides, I'm the maker of the rules, so let's dance." They made their way onto the crowded floor and fell into step with the music. Alison danced well, matching her movements to his. Matt looked down at her happy, laughing face and tried to smile back. When the music changed to a slow song, he thought about getting back to the table.

"Oh, I love this song," Alison sighed.

Matt groaned inwardly and kept on dancing, holding her lightly in his arms, thinking of the last time he'd been on a dance floor. He remembered what it was like to hold Molly, and the memory made him ache. Looking over Alison's head, he saw Molly at the table. She was leaning across Krista, talking to Brent, her face full of life and energy.

At that moment she looked up at him; her face changed and grew serious. Matt felt as if he were being drawn into her eyes. He couldn't stop staring at her. He thought back to his abrupt entrance into the party that afternoon and remembered Molly holding the lingerie against her body. He didn't know what the lacy red thing was, but it had sent him into a fantasy world where Molly was wearing it—and nothing else.

He stumbled badly. "Sorry, Alison. I'm not much of a dancer...."

"One misstep doesn't make a bad dancer, Matt. You were doing so well."

"That's what you say," he told her with a forced laugh, "but I'd rather sit it out for a while. Let me buy you a drink in apology for stepping on your toes."

Despite her protests, Matt took Alison's elbow and led her back to the table.

MOLLY DANCED WITH PETE and with Brent. She laughed and talked and joked with the crowd at the table. All of this should make her have a good time. After all, she was about to pull off the wedding of the year. But Matt Kincaid kept invading her thoughts. He seemed to dominate the whole table as a powerful presence.

She knew he was watching her. She could feel the heat of his gaze across the table, causing her to experience a kind of excited anticipation. She was glad he hadn't asked her to dance because the memory of their last dance was too strong. She remembered the feeling of being in his arms, his body against to hers.

"What the hell am I doing?" she muttered to herself. "I'm being a fool."

Pete leaned close. "Bad sign, Molly, babe, when you talk to to yourself. Even worse when you answer your own questions."

"I was just thinking out loud."

"That's what I mean," he teased.

She tried to ignore him, but it was impossible.

"Wanna dance again?"

"Not now," she replied.

"Then monopolize Brent for a while so I can dance with Krista."

"No!" she cried far too loudly. Several people turned to look at her. Molly smiled at them weakly then turned back to Pete and whispered a warning into his ear. "You are not to dance with Krista, and I mean it."

"Not even once?"

"Not even once."

"What harm can it do?"

"I'm not sure, but I imagine a lot more than you know." Molly pushed away from the table. "I'm going to get something to drink." When she reached the bar, she ordered a soft drink. She decided to take it outside. What she really needed was a breath of fresh air.

Molly inhaled the scents of the damp night and leaned against the fender of a pickup truck parked near the entrance. The Buckaroo sign flashed green and red and cast an eerie glow across the gravel parking lot.

Then a white light appeared from behind her as the door to the club opened and Matt stepped outside. Was that what she'd been waiting for, hoping for?

"Are you enjoying the party?"

"Very much. How about you?"

"It's okay. If you like noise, smoke and bad music." He put his hand on her arm, and she jumped at his touch.

"Molly, what's the matter?"

"Nothing," she lied.

"Then let's get out of here."

"No, we can't . . . the party. . ." she began.

"They'll never miss us."

"My coat, my purse. . ."

"Walenski will take care of them."

Before she could protest further, he propelled her toward his Jeep. He opened the door and Molly climbed in.

Matt joined her. "You've been avoiding me."

He was very close to her. The front seat seemed filled with him, the length of his legs, the breadth of his shoulders. He took her hand in his. "What's going on, Molly?"

She was silent for a long moment. "That sounds like a simple question, but the answer is difficult. I'm confused—"

"Me, too."

Her eyes widened in surprise. "You—the intrepid, know-it-all Matt Kincaid, confused?"

"You confused me and dumbfounded me and made me crazy from the first minute I saw you. But you know all that." He smoothed a curl from her forehead. "I have other thoughts about you that aren't at all confused. In fact, they're unmistakably carnal. I want you, Molly. More than you can imagine." He leaned toward her.

Molly backed away. "For a weekend in Tahiti? For a fling, a convenient excuse to call off the wedding?"

He narrowed his eyes thoughtfully. "You still believe that?"

"Oh, Matt, I don't know what to believe."

"Believe *me*." He reached for her and drew her close. "And believe this. I can't stop thinking about you. About what it was like to make love to you. I want you all the time, and when I saw you at the shower, holding that red lacy thing against your body, it made me crazy, Molly."

He lowered his mouth to hers. Molly closed her eyes as their breaths mingled, tongues touching. Molly felt herself flow into the kiss, losing all her tenseness and anxiety in Matt's arms. She was caught up in the feel and taste of him, the way his arms held her and his mouth claimed hers. A warm heat began to surge through her, making her feel vibrant and alive again. When his hand caressed her breast through the fabric of her sweater, Molly writhed beneath his touch.

She knew exactly what she wanted.

"You're right," she whispered. "No one at the party is going to miss us. Let's go home."

THE HOUSE WAS STILL, dark and silent around them. Molly and Matt stood in the hallway kissing, their bodies molded tightly against each other. The ride home had been quiet and anticipatory as Molly held on to his hand for dear life, no thoughts in her mind but to be with him again, to touch him, to love him.

Now it was happening. His mouth met hers in a hot and demanding kiss. Cupping her bottom with his hands he pulled her hips against his. She felt his arousal, hard and erect. Molly felt herself grow weak with desire and wondered if she could even walk up the stairs.

Maybe they'd have to make love right here, on the floor. She didn't care.

His breath was warm against her lips. "My bed or yours?"

"Yours, this time." But could she get there?

Matt had the answer when he picked her up in one strong motion and started for the stairs.

Molly hid her head against his shoulder. "I feel just like Scarlett in *Gone with the Wind*. Remember when Rhett carried her up those stairs?"

Matt laughed. "I remember, but she wasn't very willing, was she?"

"No," Molly concurred.

"How about you?" They were on the landing. "Any objections?"

Molly shook her head just before kissing him. "None at all."

Matt strode down the hall, kicked open the door to his room and laid her down on the bed. When he turned on the lamp, its light painted the room in a golden glow. Molly was only vaguely aware of an antique brass bed, a tall chest of drawers and a desk piled high with papers and books. But she was very aware of Matt. He'd pulled off his boots and sat on the bed beside her, his hand fumbling for the buttons on her shirt.

"I'm going to be very disappointed if you're not wearing that lacy thing...."

Molly kicked off her shoes and then watched as he finished undressing her.

"Oh, yes," he breathed as she lay naked before him in the teddy. He moved his hands along its silky smoothness. "You *did* wear it." He laid his cheek on the soft material that stretched over her abdomen.

Molly ran her fingers through his thick hair and inhaled the scent of him. It made her head spin.

"Did you wear it for me?" he asked.

"Yes, for you."

He lifted his head and looked at her. "It's delectable. You're delectable. Thank goodness for lingerie showers...."

He leaned forward and traced the line of her collarbone with his tongue and then kissed the hollow between her breasts.

Molly moaned and closed her eyes. Her head was still swimming, and her skin felt tight and taut. She ached with need for him.

Matt moved his mouth to her breast, and through the soft silk and lace, he teased her nipple with his tongue. "This is a marvelous little piece of clothing, Molly. But I'm going to take it off of you, inch by inch. Just lie back, my love, and relax."

Relaxation was the furthest thing from Molly's mind. She was vitally alive, her body singing with passion. But she willed herself to stay calm and let Matt do what he wanted.

He pulled the strap of her teddy down her arm, exposing her breast. His lips found the nipple and he nibbled tenderly. Then he freed the other breast, caressing her nipple with his fingers while he continued to work magic with his mouth. Molly gave up all attempts to relax and writhed beneath him.

His slow, leisurely removal of the teddy was torment, but the torture was exquisite. Carefully he lifted her hips and pulled the garment over her stomach to her thighs. Then he sat up and with gentle hands worked it down her legs and pulled it off. The teddy lay crumpled on his bed like the discarded petals of an exotic jungle flower.

Then his mouth sought her bare flesh and kissed, licked and loved until she was on fire. "Now, Matt . . ." Her mouth was dry and the words caught in her throat. She licked her lips and swallowed hard before saying the rest. "Now I'm going to love you." She reached for his zipper and pulled his jeans down.

"I've made it easy for you, Molly. Nothing under my jeans."

Nothing but his hard arousal waited for her. "Let me love you, Matt. Let me love you the way you love me. I've been waiting . . ." Again her words faded as she kissed his mouth, his neck, his flat brown nipples while her hand held on to his erection. Finally she kissed him there, too. She wanted to love every part of him.

Matt groaned and reached for her. "You're driving me crazy, Molly. I can't wait another minute."

She was open and ready, and when he entered her, he filled her totally, completely. They began to move together in perfect harmony, slowly at first and then more frantically as mutual desire overwhelmed them. Molly looked at his face above her and was filled with an emotion so powerful it took her breath away. She smiled and then laughed aloud as she gave herself to the spasms of fulfillment that washed over her in undulating waves, one building on the other.

"PERFECTION AGAIN," Matt murmured against her ear.

She tried to respond but words didn't come.

"Molly?"

"Hmm?" That's all she could manage.

"Wasn't it perfection?"

"Umm."

He leaned up on one elbow and looked down at her. "Tell me in words of more than half a syllable."

"I'll try," she said with a lazy laugh.

"I want to hear just what you're thinking."

"I'm not sure I can find my voice. . . ."

"You have it now."

"You took my breath away, and then it took my voice away. I'm getting them both back now," she said. "So I can tell you. It was wonderful. Too good to be true."

"Don't say that."

"You wanted me to put it in words," she replied.

"Yes, but it's not too good to be true. It *is* true. It's good and true, and it's going to happen again and again. We're going to make love just like this and even better many times. After this wedding is over—"

"What? You're admitting there's going to be a wedding?"

"I bow to the inevitable. Hell, it's only two days away." He raised her hand to his lips and kissed the palm. "As much as I hate to lose, I've lost this one. Looks like my baby sister is going to marry her childhood sweetheart. And then—" he kissed her gently on the lips "—after the nuptials, when we take off for Tahiti—"

"We're really going?"

"If you want to. I told you that the invitation had nothing to do with the wedding. Two separate issues. You chose to confuse them for your own reasons."

"I suppose I did."

"So after the wedding—"

"There's the story, the pictures, so much more work to be done."

Matt silenced her with his lips.

"But Matt—"

"Just shut up, Molly. We'll figure it out."

She did as she was told.

"Now, I feel a real need," he said with a sly smile, "to continue where we left off."

Molly opened her mouth under his and flowed into his kiss.

Suddenly from somewhere downstairs a sound interrupted their tranquillity. It was loud, something between a cry and a wail, calling Matt's name.

"What in the world?" Matt sat up in bed.

"Matt," the voice called out again, "where are you? Please come down, Matt."

"It's Krista," Molly said as she sat up.

With an abrupt expletive, Matt got out of bed and reached for his jeans. "I don't know what the hell has happened," he said over his shoulder to Molly, "but you'd better put your clothes on."

Matt stalked out onto the second-floor landing. "Krista, what is it? You're yelling like a banshee."

She stood at the bottom of the stairs, her eyes swollen from crying, her whole body shaking.

Matt took the steps two at a time and grabbed his trembling sister. "All right, sis. Just calm down and tell me what's the matter."

Molly hastily dressed and came out onto the landing, buttoning her blouse. She took in the scene and quickly descended the stairs.

Krista was still sobbing.

"Has there been an accident?" Molly asked.

"Yes. Well, no. I mean, Pete's in the emergency room."

Molly gasped. "Oh, no. Is he all right?"

"Just tell us what happened," Matt calmly instructed his sister.

"It was Brent. I danced with Pete—"

"Dammit," Molly swore. "I warned him—"

Matt shook his head at Molly. "Doesn't matter. Go on, sis."

"I danced with Pete. Just one dance, not even a whole dance, really because—" She started sobbing again.

Matt gave her a gentle shake. "Go ahead, Krista."

"Well Brent got really mad. He pushed Pete and then Pete started to walk away but Brent went after him. Some of the guys tried to hold him back. The manager came out and told him to stop, but Brent got away and grabbed Pete. I'm not sure what happened next."

She started to sob again but got hold of herself. "I think Pete tried to push Brent away. That's when Brent hit him. Pete fell back and banged his head on the edge of the table. Oh, it was terrible. He had a real gash, and it just bled and bled. They tried to stop it with napkins, but the manager was really upset. He called an ambulance and the police and—"

Molly sank down on the steps. "Oh, no," she moaned.

"Is he all right?" Matt asked.

Krista answered between sobs. "The paramedics came and bandaged him up, and they said he'd be fine. But there was so much blood—"

"Where is he now?"

"They took him to the hospital to get stitches."

"This can't be real. It can't be happening," Molly murmured, shaking her head.

"What about Brent?" Matt asked.

"He's at the police station," she wailed. "They took him away, and I came home to find you."

"That was just what you should have done, sis. It's going to be all right. I'll put on some clothes and drive you down to the police station. We'll get Brent out. Unless Walenski decides to press charges—"

Molly got to her feet. "He won't," she said grimly. "Pete will cause no more problems, trust me."

Matt disappeared upstairs. Krista watched him go, his state of undress finally making an impression on her. "Oh, I'm so sorry. You and Matt—I didn't mean—"

Molly hugged Krista. "It's okay. Everything'll be fine. We'll straighten this mess out, and tomorrow things will seem very different. You'll see. This won't stop the wedding, so don't worry, Krista."

Krista nodded wearily. "Will you call the hospital and make sure Pete's all right?"

"I'll go there myself. If I can borrow a car."

Again, Krista nodded dully. "I drove Brent's car home. It's outside."

"Keys?" Molly asked.

"They're in the car, your coat and purse, too. We just threw in everything that was left at the club. The manager was pretty upset. I guess he wanted us all out of there. But we left Pete's Jeep—"

"That's all right," Molly said. "I'll take care of it. Somehow." She wasn't quite sure how. "I'll take care of everything," she repeated with more assurance than she felt. "It'll all work out fine."

AFTER KRISTA AND MATT left, Molly called the Buckaroo and told the distraught manager that she'd have Pete's Jeep picked up the next morning. Stitches or no stitches, she'd see that Pete got over and retrieved it. Now that she knew he was all right, she felt less than sympathetic toward her photographer. He should have known better.

At the hospital, Molly identified herself and tried to get information about Pete. "If you'll just sit down over there," the reception-desk nurse told her, indicating an area of worn-looking chairs. "I'll check with the doctor and see if you can visit the patient."

"Is he all right?" Molly asked with less concern than she really felt at the moment. "Will he have to spend the night?"

The nurse gave Molly a tired look, as if she'd answered the same questions a hundred times that night.

"Doctor will have to tell you that." Then she softened her words with a smile. "It won't be long."

Molly sat back and tried to relax. She managed with some success until she caught a glimpse of herself in the waiting-room window. The harsh greenish glow of fluorescent lights did nothing to enhance her image, which was pretty awful to begin with. She looked as if she'd been in an accident of some kind. Her hair bushed wildly around her face and her skin was eerily pale in the bad lighting.

Horrified, Molly fumbled around in her purse for her makeup bag. She brushed her hair vigorously, put on lipstick and blush, and then sat back, again breathing deeply, trying to get her jumbled emotions under control. One moment she and Matt had been in bed; the next moment she'd been driving to the emergency room. The evening had taken on a kind of surrealist quality with images blurred together in a bizarre, unreal and frightening manner.

She was ready for a little logic. It came in the person of the nurse, an extrememly solid, practical-looking woman who adressed her openly. "Ms. Prescott, the doctor has completed her examination of Mr. Walenski, and you may see him now."

"Is the doctor still there?" Molly wanted an explanation from someone other than Pete.

"Yes, she is. Down the corridor, the last room on the right."

Pete was sitting on the edge of the bed, a large butterfly bandage across his temple. He looked pale and drawn, but otherwise like the same old Pete, calm and not in the slightest concerned about his situation. He raised a couple of fingers in greeting. It was the cool that had gotten him through violent demonstrations, riots, even wars. It served him quite well in this situation, which was far less dramatic than a war but, as far as Molly was concerned, no less important.

"Are you all right?"

"Except for the damage to my male ego, I'm fine. The guy didn't take me down, Molly. I must impress that upon you. I slipped on the beer-drenched floor."

"I'm not in the mood for a macho act, Pete."

"Just an explanation. In fact, I tried to keep from fighting him."

"But not from dancing with his fiancée. Oh, never mind," Molly said wearily. "When can you get out of here?"

"Whenever the good doctor says. Hey, Doc, when can you spring me?"

The doctor completed Pete's chart and looked up with a nod to Molly. "No signs of concussion, but he needs to be watched for the next twelve hours—either here or..." She looked at Molly. "Will you be able to stay with him?"

"I guess I have no choice."

"How gracious," Pete joked.

"Then I can sign him out." The doctor gave Molly a sheet of instructions about what to watch for while Pete went to the desk to take care of his bill.

They were out of the hospital and into Pete's hotel room in less than half an hour, but Molly still felt as though she was caught in some surreal dimension.

There was a quality to the evening that was like a dream, or maybe even a nightmare. She chould only hope that morning would bring a return to normalcy.

She settled Pete on the bed and tried to reach Krista or Matt, but there was no answer. She left a message saying she would be staying with Pete and then stretched out on the twin bed next to his and read over the instructions.

"What's the deal?"

"I have to wake you up every couple of hours."

"Absurd. I've had head injuries before with no problems, and certainly no one nursing me through the night."

"Well, this time it's different, and this time you have a nurse, like it or not. I don't plan for you to die on us in spite of your behavior."

"Molly, I didn't touch the guy. In fact, I tried to stay away from him."

"You danced with Krista after I specifically asked you not to. That's what created the problem, as you well know." Molly didn't even try to keep the anger out of her voice.

"Some gentle loving nurse you are," Pete grumbled, his eyes closed.

"What in the world were you thinking of?"

Pete lay still. "I was thinking that this might be the last chance I'd have to dance with her. I was thinking that she was marrying the wrong man, that she and I belonged together."

"Well, you were thinking wrong. She belongs with Brent, and that's who she'll be marrying in two days so you might as well get over this fantasy."

"Do you believe in love at first sight, Molly?"

"No. And neither do you. You believe in love at every glance. I've seen you operate, Pete, so don't try to con me."

"This is different. I've never felt anything like it before."

"It's lust, Pete, not love."

"Shows what you know. What I feel for Krista is different—it's very special. Things like this happen, Molly. And it's happened to us, to me and Krista."

"Leave Krista out of this," Molly ordered.

Pete opened his eyes and smiled sadly. "Poor Molly. You only see what you want to see." He sighed deeply and then closed his eyes again. "Hey, can you turn out the light?"

Molly reached over and snapped off the bedside lamp.

"Thanks. And thanks for hanging out here even though you don't need to."

"It's okay."

"You're a real pal. And I understand what you have to do, Molly. So you can go ahead and get it over with."

"What are you talking about?"

"Molly, you know very well."

"No, I don't."

"You're going to fire me from this shoot."

Molly took a deep breath. She'd been trying to avoid it, but Peter wasn't going to let her. "I thought we'd talk in the morning when you feel better."

In the dim light, Pete looked at her wordlessly.

"Well, I—"

"Go on, Molly."

"Don't you see? I can't have you at the wedding, not after this. It would be too disruptive and upsetting, not only to Brent, but to Krista. You have to think of her."

"I am thinking of her."

"I don't mean like that. You know what I'm talking about, and I'm sure you understand. You're a professional, after all."

He laughed softly. "Sometimes. So who's going to take your photos?"

Molly hadn't thought that far. "I'll call the local paper. I'm sure they'll have someone on staff who freelances. It'll only be for the ceremony. You've done everything else—the house, the town, all the parties, Krista from every angle, of course."

He smiled.

"I'll work it out."

"Yeah, that's our Molly. Always in control."

Pete grew quiet then, and soon Molly drifted off to sleep with his words still in her head. Rather than comforting her, they'd left her with a strange sense of foreboding.

MATT WAS IN THE KITCHEN when Molly arrived at the Kincaid house early the next morning. He looked as tired as she felt.

"Oh, Matt—"

He opened his arms, and she stepped willingly into them. "What a night you must have had."

"It's been awful for all of us, and I'm sorry, Matt."

He kissed her gently. "Don't be sorry. It's not your fault."

"But Pete—"

"From what I understand, it wasn't his fault, either."

"Well, I've fired him."

Matt stepped back. "Do you think that was necessary?"

"Absolutely. He's a disruptive influence any way you look at it."

"I suppose you're right. Maybe things will calm down now."

"How's Brent?"

"Out of jail and at home."

"And Krista?"

"Upstairs. She and Brent were up until all hours talking. She must be exhausted, too."

"Is everything all right?"

"As far as I know." He gave her a squeeze. "How about you?"

"Tired but hanging in there. It's Krista I'm worried about."

She appeared at the door just as her name was mentioned. She looked pale but controlled, and Molly couldn't help thinking she was more beautiful than ever, although cooler and more aloof, like an ice princess.

"Don't worry. I can take care of myself," Krista said quietly.

"I wouldn't have thought so last night," Matt answered.

Molly shot him a silencing look. "Of course you can take care of yourself," she assured her. "But so close to the wedding, every bride gets a little jittery."

Krista pulled her jacket off a peg near the door. "Don't patronize me, Molly."

"I wasn't." She paused. "Sorry, I guess I was."

Krista slipped into the jacket.

"Where're you going?" Matt asked.

"To the store," was her curt reply.

"So early?"

"We have a shipment to unpack."

"Can't Diane or Alison do it?" Molly asked. "You really should get some rest." Krista gave her an icy stare, and Molly backed down. "Sorry again. I'm sure you know best."

Pausing at the door, Krista replied, "I'm just beginning to realize that." Then she went out and shut the door behind her.

Matt and Molly stood looking at each other. "Whew," he breathed, trying to lighten the mood. "I believe an iceberg disguised as my sister just floated through."

"Trust me, all brides go through it. Wedding nerves. I call it the wedding bell blues syndrome. As soon as she puts on that dress and walks down the aisle..." She saw the look of concern on Matt's face. "You haven't changed your mind about the wedding again?"

He shook his head.

"It really is the best thing for Krista and Brent."

"That's not my place to say, Molly, which I've finally realized. It's not yours, either."

His voice was light, but Molly heard the underlying conviction. "You're right. I'll do everything I have to do, and just hope for the best. No more advice for anyone," she added.

He leaned over and kissed her. "Now, I must remind you of our unfinished business."

She looked up, puzzled.

"Well, not exactly business. Last night? If you remember, we were very rudely interrupted."

"I'm available to take up where we left off," she said flirtatiously.

"Tonight. I have an appointment in Denver, but I'll be back this afternoon. Dinner, and—" He kissed her again.

"I like the 'and' part," she murmured. Just the thought of spending the evening alone with him sent a warm glow over her.

"In that case, I'll see you, Prescott."

"Later, Kincaid."

11

THERE WERE PLENTY of other things for Molly to be thinking about, so why was her mind filled only with Matt? It was the teddy, she decided. That had to be what was causing the problem. She'd undressed to take a shower, dropping it onto the bathroom floor. There it lay, a reminder of last night, a reminder of Matt.

She stepped into the shower and stood under the stinging jets of water, all her thoughts given over to him. She didn't even try to think of anything else; it would have been impossible. She loved him. There. She'd said it to herself, and there was no doubt about it. Of course, he didn't know, not yet. She'd tell him tonight, and they'd have a chance to talk, not about the wedding but about each other, and maybe their trip.

There was going to be a trip, Molly realized. Somehow she'd work it out with *Wedding*. For the first time, her job seemed an inconvenience. That was a strange feeling and one that would take some getting used to.

She dressed quickly and tried to return her concentration to events at hand. There was a wedding coming up, after all. Should she call New York and explain that she'd fired Pete? Molly decided against it. She'd find a replacement for the rest of the job and let them know later—if Pete didn't take it upon himself to report back to the powers-that-be.

She didn't think he would. He knew better. Molly dragged a brush through her tangled hair. She felt awful for firing him, but what else could she have done? Pete had sense enough to know that his presence at the wedding would be enough to set Brent off again, especially when combined with the way Krista had been acting. The situation was a powder keg just waiting to explode. But without Pete around, everything would go smoothly. As for the job, she'd make it all up to him with plum future assignments.

She thought about calling Pete to tell him that. It might make him feel better, but it wasn't really necessary. She'd have plenty of time to let him know when she stopped by to check on him later in the afternoon. Meanwhile, she had the keys to his Jeep and no qualms about using it for last-minute errands.

Molly checked over her handwritten list. It included a stop at the florist and the bakery, with the most important item in big letters at the top: PHOTOGRA-PHER.

The best ones would be on staff or free-lancing at the Denver *Post*. She'd briefly considered trying the local papers and decided against it. If they were really good, they'd be in Denver so she'd just have to use Pete's Jeep to get there. After all, he wasn't going anywhere today.

She called a cab to take her to the Buckaroo, where, happily, she avoided contact with the manager. She headed for Denver in Pete's Jeep, leaving Pete to recuperate at the hotel.

IT WAS MID-AFTERNOON before Molly got back, irritated with the florist and not terribly happy with the baker but pleased that at least she'd found a photographer, a young woman who was up-and-coming, according to the assignment editor at the newspaper office. A quick look at some of her work convinced Molly that while she wasn't of Pete's caliber—very few people were—she had talent. She could complete the job.

WITH PETE OUT of the picture, a new photographer ready and willing to take over, a wedding cake that was nearly—if not absolutely—perfect, and enough potted plants and cut flowers to fill every room of the house, Molly could relax at last.

She settled in the kitchen with a cup of Suzanne's tea, which she'd grown to like, and smiled to herself. It was all going to work. This really could turn out to be the wedding of the year. She had a sudden urge to see Krista, give her a big hug, reassure her.

Molly went to the phone and called Kincaid Mountaineering. The line was busy. She hung up and tried again. Still busy. Probably one of the bridesmaids talking to a girlfriend about the wedding. Spurred by her lifted spirits, she decided not to wait. She grabbed her purse and Pete's car keys and headed for the door.

Kincaid Mountaineering was full of shoppers, but Molly managed to push through to the back of the store. Krista was nowhere to be seen. A thread of panic began to snake through her. She brushed it away as she spotted Lisa waiting on a woman in the shoe department. Molly gave her a nudge and managed to pull her aside.

"Where's Krista?" she asked.

Lisa shrugged. "I don't know."

"Do you remember when she left, where she was going?"

"She hasn't been in," Lisa said, puzzled.

"At all?"

"No. Molly, my customer—"

"Lisa, this is very important. Do you have any idea where she is?"

"We thought she was probably at home resting up for the big day. We're all so excited—"

"Maybe she's with Matt," Molly interrupted.

"No, he's still in Denver."

Suddenly Molly had a terrible premonition. It was absurd, but it persisted. And it scared her to death. With a quick goodbye to Lisa, she made a mad dash for the door while startled customers stopped their shopping to watch.

THE DILLARD INN WAS on the other side of the mall, and Molly made a half-dozen wrong turns before she finally pulled up in the hotel parking lot and got out.

The desk clerk's information wasn't a surprise. "I'm sorry, Mr. Walenski has checked out."

"When did he leave? Do you remember?"

"Well—"

"Please, this is important."

"I can't remember exactly, but I believe it was right after my break. That would be about two hours ago."

"Was he alone?"

"Yes, that is, he came to the desk alone, but someone picked him up."

"Did you see who it was?"

"I'm afraid not."

Molly's sigh was audible.

"Is something the matter?"

"Oh, no. Everything's fine. No, I'm just a hard-working editor who's about to be out of a job."

The desk clerk shrugged sympathetically in reply.

Molly managed to thank him before heading back to Pete's Jeep. She climbed in and, feeling utterly powerless, drove back to the Kincaid house.

There was no sign of life. Her empty teacup was still on the table. Since she couldn't think of anything else to do, Molly went to the stove to heat water for another cup.

Then she saw the envelope on the counter. It had been there all along, but she just hadn't noticed, an ordinary business envelope addressed in Krista's handwriting to her and Matt. She ripped it open.

The first sentence was enough to confirm all Molly's suspicions. "I know you'll be shocked by what I'm going to do, but I hope you'll understand."

Did I just scream? Molly asked herself. *I couldn't have; that would have been crazy.* But something inside her head was screaming and—in her present state of mind—it was highly possible the noise had made its way to her lips. She covered them with her hand as she read the letter through once, quickly. then she collapsed in a chair and read it again, her head spinning, her breath catching in her throat and her heart pounding in her chest.

Dear Molly and Matt,

I know you'll be shocked by what I'm going to do, but I hope you'll understand. Brent and I have called off our wedding. We talked a lot about it and even though I love him dearly, I love him as a friend.

The closer we got to the wedding date, the more both of us realized that we didn't share the passionate kind of love that can bind a man and woman for a lifetime. It may seem cruel now, but I'm doing Brent a favor by not marrying him.

As for my future—remember when you said I knew best, Molly? Well, I do. I'm off on the adventure of a lifetime with a man I love madly. I think both of you can understand that feeling.

Sometimes love is so strong that it knows no right or wrong. Please don't look for us—we know what we're doing. And we'll be in touch.

Matt, I love you. You're the best brother in the world. Please be happy for me.

Molly, I'm sorry about the wedding, but there'll be others more beautiful. Please take care of Matt.

With all my love,

Krista

All Molly's worst fears had come true; she held the proof in her hand. She sat numbly, trying to think of her next move. What could she do, call the police? Obviously not. Krista and Pete were certainly of age. Maybe she could call the airlines and have the flights watched, in case they hadn't left yet. Detectives always did that in movies. Except she wasn't a detective, and this certainly wasn't a movie. It was real life.

Molly tried to gather her thoughts. What next? She could try to find Brent. No, bad idea, she told herself, trying not to imagine what Brent must be going through. There was nothing to do now but wait for Matt.

Nearly an hour later, she heard him turn into the driveway and breathed a sigh of relief. Matt would know what to do.

"Molly, are you all right?" he asked as he walked into the kitchen. "You look like something awful has happened." He bent down to kiss her.

"Actually it has." Molly handed him the note, and suddenly she began to tremble.

He read it once quickly, just as she had, and then in disbelief read it again, swearing under his breath. "She's run off with Walenski."

"What can we do? I went by the hotel. He left over two hours ago. Krista never went to work at all." Molly ran through her pitiful string of ideas again. "Should we check the airlines or call the police? Maybe they could put out an all-points bulletin, or something," she added pathetically.

Matt looked at her as if she'd lost her mind. "Prescott, Krista is a grown woman. She made a decision, no matter how crazy, and there's nothing we can do about it."

"Couldn't you track her down? You must know some favorite place she might go. Maybe you could get a plea on television for her to come home."

"You're missing the point, Prescott." Matt dropped into a chair. "I was right all along. Krista wasn't ready to get married. All these preparations scared her to death, and she reacted by running away. Damn, damn!" He beat his fist on the table.

Molly looked up at him in surprise. She'd never seen Matt so hurt—or angry—and the anger seemed to be directed at her. She moved away from him. For a moment when he'd driven up Molly'd had a fantasy that they would be together, in each other's arms, giving comfort, working out a plan to get Krista back. But Matt obviously wasn't in the mood to comfort or to cooperate with her.

"I don't think it was anxiety over the wedding," she defended. "I think it was Pete."

"The bastard." Matt almost spat out the word. "He comes into my house, seduces my sister, spirits her away—"

"Now just a minute, Kincaid. You just got through saying Krista is a grown woman perfectly able to make her own choices. Her note didn't sound as if she were being spirited away. It sounded very much as if she went willingly. It could very well have been her idea."

"No, Prescott, it was Walenski's idea, and you know it. Krista was vulnerable, that's all."

Molly made an attempt to speak, but he cut her off.

"And don't try to shy away from your responsibility. You forced the issue of this wedding, which deep in her heart my sister didn't want—"

"She wrote to *Wedding*, Kincaid. I didn't pursue her."

"But once you got here, you were on her like a shark."

Molly's concern over Krista suddenly turned to a livid, white-hot anger. "A shark! I was only doing what I thought Krista and Brent wanted. At least, it was what they said they wanted. They were supposedly in love, and—"

"I told you from the beginning they weren't."

"And we've had this conversation from the beginning. There's no use going over it again and again."

Matt stood up and faced her. "You're right about that, Prescott. There's no use going over it because you won't listen. You never have listened. You've been too busy feathering your own nest, thinking of your career and the big story for that magazine of yours. If you'd have used your eyes and ears for one minute instead of plowing ahead like a steamroller, you'd have seen what was happening."

"First a shark and then a steamroller," Molly shouted. "Can't you be more inventive, Kincaid? You've used steamroller. As far as I'm concerned I was only an editor doing my job."

"Right. And thinking nothing about the people involved."

Molly bristled, fighting back. "Your tactics weren't so subtle either, if you remember. You did everything in your power to try and stop the wedding, and with what results? You convinced Krista that marriage to Brent was a mistake and so she ran off with Pete. If anyone's to blame it's you. If you'd stayed out of it, Krista would be here and we'd have a wedding to put on."

"It always gets back to that wedding, doesn't it, Prescott? That's all you've cared about since you got here."

For a moment Molly felt her body slump. Maybe he was right, maybe she was nothing but an opportunist looking for a way to further her career.

No, that wasn't true; Molly knew it. Quickly she regained her composure and stood up straight to face him squarely. She wasn't about to buy into Matt's accusations. She cared for Krista just as he did, and they'd both made the same mistake. In caring, they'd tried to make decisions for her that Krista was perfectly capable of handling herself.

"What you say isn't true," she told him. "I cared about Krista and Brent. And dammit, I cared about you, as you very well know."

Matt looked at her for a long hard minute. "I don't know anything, Prescott, except that my sister has gone off with a guy she just met, and I have no idea where she is or what she's doing."

"I guess if she'd wanted you to know, she would have told you. Maybe she's tired of big brother interfering in her life. Maybe this was the only way she could get away from you." She stopped, and briefly closed her eyes. "And from me, too, I guess."

Matt didn't seem to hear the admission. "If I could get my hands on Walenski now, I'd kill him."

"Well, you can't get your hands on him, and neither can I. As for killing him, you'd better think twice about that. Pete may end up being your brother-in-law."

Matt sat back down, looking emotionally exhausted. "How could this have happened? You knew Walenski, yet you let him come here, get involved with Krista—"

"As soon as I saw what was happening, I tried to keep him away. Hell, I fired him. What more could I have done?"

"Told me what was going on. I could have handled him."

"Then why didn't you use *your* eyes and ears?" Molly said, throwing back the words he'd used earlier. "In fact, I think you secretly liked Pete flirting with Krista. You were in favor of anything that drove a wedge between her and Brent. All your talk about how Brent was wrong for her finally paid off. Now she's gone, and we have no idea where she is."

"I knew Krista wasn't herself this morning. She probably left here and went straight to Walenski. If you'd let me go after her—"

"Let you go after her? When have you ever needed to ask my permission? You're a grown man. You—"

They both heard the car pull up. Matt strode to the window. "Suzanne and Brent. Bad news spreads fast."

Molly covered her face with her hands. "I don't know how I can face them."

Matt reached for his coat. "Well, you better think of something, Prescott, because I'm out of here. You came into our lives like a—"

"Steamroller," Molly finished for him sarcastically.

"Exactly. Now you can deal with the debris."

"You're leaving me alone with them? You're running out on me?"

"I'm not running out. I'm going for a long drive in the mountains. I have a lot of thinking to do."

Matt stepped out the door, and Molly saw him stop to talk briefly with Brent and Suzanne before getting into his Jeep.

Molly stood morosely in the doorway waiting for Brent and his mother. She held her head high and tried to control her trembling knees.

When they approached she moved forward. "Here I am. Yell at me. Hit me. Give me your best shot. I know you think it's all my fault, too." Her voice trembled a little on the last words.

To her amazement, Brent hugged her. "It's rough, isn't it, Molly?"

"Rough? It's a nightmare. But how did you know?"

Suzanne began bustling around the kitchen as if it were her own. "I'm serving drinks," she announced. "Herbal tea, coffee..."

She didn't get any takers.

"There's also a half bottle of wine, and I know where Matt keeps the Scotch. Now order up," Suzanne prompted.

"Tea," Molly mumbled. "With a shot of Scotch in it."

Suzanne laughed. "I'll have the same but without the tea."

"Nothing for me," Brent said evenly. "I'm fine."

Molly looked at him through widened eyes. "You're fine?"

Brent shrugged. "It's amazing what a few hours in jail and a broken engagement can do for you." He sat down at the table and stretched out his legs. "It's a freeing kind of experience."

Suzanne handed Molly a glass. "It's Scotch. I decided you didn't need any tea, either."

Molly took a sip and choked. The Scotch burned a trail down her throat. She blinked hard and looked from Brent to Suzanne, who'd joined them at the table. "You don't hate me?"

"Did you aid and abet Krista and Pete?" Suzanne asked.

"Of course not."

"Then why should we hate you?"

Molly shrugged, unable to answer. Then she took another taste of her drink. "I wanted the wedding to go off more than anyone," she said fervently.

Molly thought she saw Suzanne and Brent exchange glances.

"Matt says I wanted it for my career. Do you think that?"

"Of course not," Suzanne assured her.

"Brent, I really thought you and Krista were perfect for each other," Molly explained. "I wanted you to be happy."

"We were perfect—no, we are perfect," Brent corrected. "Perfect friends. She'll always be my best friend. But never my wife," he added with a sad smile. "When I saw her with Walenski, hell, even I knew. She never looked at me like that. She loved me, but she was wildly in love with him. That's why I went so crazy at the club. Just seeing them dancing—it was so damned obvious."

"Sometimes we try to ignore the obvious, don't we?" Suzanne asked.

Molly had a feeling the question was directed at her, too.

"I'm glad we found out before the wedding," Brent went on. "I'm not denying that I'm hurt and jealous—or that I'm embarrassed at being left at the altar—but consider the alternatives. What if we'd gotten married even though she wasn't really in love with me? Eventually someone like Walenski would have turned up. What then?" He smiled at Molly. "Things have a way of working out. My wounded pride will heal eventually."

"I just can't believe you're so...so calm," Molly said.

"Krista and I talked for a long time last night. I guess I'm in a state of emotional exhaustion now."

"You knew last night and yet you didn't say anything. You didn't tell us what she was planing to do. Why didn't you call and warn us?"

Brent smiled. "I didn't know. But I suspected she might run off just to get everyone out of her hair. Oops, sorry, Molly."

Molly shrugged.

"But Krista is still my best friend. I'd never have given away her secret, even if I'd known for sure."

Molly sighed. "What a mess."

"Not necessarily," Suzanne contradicted. "Krista has always wanted to see more of the world. I expect she'll be doing that now. And she'll find out for herself if Pete is the man for her."

Molly thought about that for a long moment. "I've seen Pete flirt, certainly. And often. But I've never seen him so serious about anyone. Maybe it just might work."

"I hope so," Suzanne said. "As for my son, he's strong, smart, and quite handsome if I do say so myself. There'll be another woman in his life. When it's time. Take it from one who knows, Molly, timing is everything, and the timing was just off for Brent and Krista."

"And for me," Molly added. "At the risk of sounding selfish, I do have a wedding scheduled for the day after tomorrow, and there's not a bride in sight." She focused on Suzanne. "Is there someone you'd like to walk down the aisle with?"

Suzanne threw back her head and laughed. Brent joined in, and finally Molly began laughing, a little hysterically, but it was better than crying.

"Nope, once is enough for me. Maybe you could do a story about what really happened."

"I'm afraid that wouldn't work. It's called *Wedding* magazine, remember."

With that they all started laughing again.

"Maybe you could put out a supplement, 'Left at the Altar'," Brent suggested, and the laughter escalated.

Finally, Suzanne grew serious. "This will cause problems, won't it?"

Molly nodded.

"Could any of the other stories be lengthened to fill up the space?"

"There wouldn't be enough copy or pictures. Besides, it's not just filling up space. This wedding was going to be a big splash, so fabulous, so perfect. Now I'll be lucky if I'm not fired."

Brent was concerned. "They wouldn't do that?"

"They might. I don't think anyone has ever messed up so royally. No photographer. No bride. No wedding! Plus, I've run up all kinds of bills. They'll have to be paid even if there isn't a wedding."

"They can't blame you if the bride changed her mind," Brent asserted.

"Oh, no?"

Suzanne was aghast. "You're serious, aren't you? You could get fired?"

"No doubt about it."

"I guess loyalty doesn't mean very much anymore," Suzanne said sadly.

"I've been loyal to them," Molly answered. "But you're right, it doesn't mean much." She was too embarrassed to tell Suzanne that she hadn't even dared inform the editor about what had happened, which was proof that she was scared about what the reaction would be. Her job was probably history.

Suzanne and Brent got to their feet. "We'll help out any way we can," Brent promised. "I'll write a letter and explain everything, if you think that'll help."

Molly shook her head. "Thanks, Brent. But I'm afraid I'll have to try and get out of this one myself. I appreciate your concern, though. It seems so strange, you're trying to cheer me up when it should be the other way around. I can't believe you're taking it so calmly."

"I'm probably just in shock," Brent said with a sad smile.

He was still trying to joke even though Molly could see the pain. Yet Suzanne was right. He'd get over it in time. Molly gave him a big hug. "Are you sure she won't come back? Maybe—"

Brent shook his head. "Not a chance."

Molly looked at Suzanne.

"No, Molly, she won't come back, at least not for a while. Krista has the wanderlust, just as I told you."

"I know. I was just hoping."

"It's not going to happen," Brent repeated. "I know you don't want to believe that. Neither does Matt. He was angry when I tried to tell him—"

"He's angry at me, not you," Molly said. "He thinks I caused all the problems. I doubt if he'll ever speak to me again, never mind forgive me. You two have just as much right to be upset as Matt, but he's—" Molly broke off. It was too difficult to talk about.

"You don't get it, do you?" Suzanne asked in amusement.

"Get what?"

"We're not upset with you because we're not in love with you."

"In love with me? Matt?" Molly blurted out. "Uh uh. No way."

Brent tried to explain. "Matt's not an emotional guy. He's always been real cool and calm. Especially about women. I've seen him plenty of times. They fall all over him, and he acts as though he doesn't even know they're there."

"Oh, he knows I'm here all right," Molly said sarcastically.

"I've never seen anyone do to him what you do, Molly. Krista and I have talked about it. I think he's angry because there's so much emotion between you two. The poor guy's struggling to get a handle on it."

"Doesn't that sound philosophical?" Suzanne asked. "But I have to agree with Brent. The opposite of love isn't anger, Molly. It's indifference, and in no way is Matt Kincaid indifferent to you. I've known Matt for years, and I've never seen a woman who could do to him what you do. It's obvious he's wild over you. He'll come home, and when he does, you two will work it out."

12

SUZANNE'S WORDS PLAYED over and over in Molly's head. She tried to ignore them and concentrate on the most pressing problem: what to do about the wedding—or the non-wedding. There really was nothing *to* do except call it all off, cancel everything. But at this hour, even that wasn't possible. She'd have to wait until morning to give the suppliers the news.

She didn't have to worry about the wedding party since Brent had probably called the groomsmen already. Most likely the phone lines were buzzing with the news to the bridesmaids. In fact, the Kincaid phone had already begun to ring. Molly ignored it. She wasn't in the mood to think about the news, much less talk about it.

Feeling very confused, useless and alone, she pulled on her jacket and went out on the porch. The night was clear and bright with thousands of stars twinkling all around her, almost close enough to touch, it seemed. Somehow, that made Molly feel even more alone.

The air was cold, but the chill didn't bother her. It seemed to complement the icy ache in her heart. With all the bad news, what hurt most was losing Matt. And she *had* lost him—there didn't seem to be any doubt about that—lost him so soon after she'd admitted her love for him, to herself at least. Now she'd never have the chance to tell him how she'd felt—how she still felt. If only things could have worked out differently....

The headlights from Matt's Jeep swept across the lawn and lit the porch where she stood. She thought of going in to avoid him and then decided against it. They'd have to face each other again before she left.

Matt came up the stairs. "What are you doing out here, Molly?"

"Looking at the stars." She managed to keep her voice from shaking.

He stood beside her. "They are beautiful, aren't they?"

His voice was gentle, without the anger she'd heard in it earlier, and that helped Molly relax a little. "I read once that there're more stars in the sky than grains of sand on all the beaches in the world. That seems amazing. Do you suppose it could be true?" She looked up at him but in the darkness couldn't read the expression on his face.

"All I know is that when I'm alone on a mountaintop, the sky seems literally filled with stars, billions of them."

They were both quiet until Matt broke the silence. "I used to tell myself that it was exciting and macho to be alone with the stars, the wind and the snow. I didn't need anyone. I was Matt Kincaid. I was invincible. That's what I used to think."

"And now?"

"Now I see that I was just another lonely guy on top of a mountain." He put his arm around Molly, who stood stiffly, not knowing how to react as he continued to talk. "I think being alone so often, no matter where you are, can be damaging."

"What do you mean?" she asked, looking up at him.

"It can keep a man from knowing how to act, even to the point that he causes pain without meaning to."

Molly was quiet.

"I shouldn't have left you alone with Suzanne and Brent."

"It's all right."

"No, it's not, Molly. I was thinking of myself, of my own reaction to what's happened. There're others involved besides me."

"Well, Suzanne and Brent seem to be doing fine. Better than—"

"Better than you?"

"Yes," she agreed. "This really has knocked me off my feet, Matt, in more ways than you know."

"I think I do know because I feel the same. That is, if you're talking about us, Molly, me and you." He touched her chin with his fingertips and tilted her head up. "Is that what you're saying?"

"Yes," she replied softly.

"It's what I've been thinking of, too. Once I cooled down, I realized so much. For one thing, I envy Pete and Krista."

"You envy them?" Molly was incredulous.

"They're off on the adventure of their lives—and they have each other. They'll never be lonely."

"So you don't hate Pete?" she asked. And then in a softer voice, "Or me?"

"Oh, Molly. Molly." He pulled her close. "How could I ever hate you? I love you."

The words were so unexpected that Molly didn't know how to respond. She'd meant to tell him that *she* loved *him*, and now—when she thought everything was over between them—he'd been the first to say the words.

"You're the only woman I've ever met who made me realize what being alone was all about."

"Matt—"

"No, let me finish. Being alone is being without you. I knew that when I got in the Jeep this afternoon and drove away."

He held her so tightly that she could hardly breathe, but it didn't matter. She was where she wanted to be. She felt tears well up in her eyes. "I'm sorry I caused all this mess," she whispered.

He released her a little so he could look down at her. "You didn't cause anything. Krista and Brent and Pete did it all themselves. Hell, I just needed someone to blame when I realized my baby sister was all grown up and didn't need me anymore. So I blamed you."

"I did a little blaming myself," she admitted.

"Apologies all around, Molly." He kissed her gently.

"Accepted," she murmured against his lips. As they stood wrapped in each other's arms, paying no attention to the cold, all Molly could think about was that he loved her. He loved her! She wanted to tell him how she felt, but before she had a chance he had a question for her.

"So what's next, Molly?"

"Well . . ."

"The canceled wedding, your job—"

"I guess I'll have to call the magazine and tell them I can't find a replacement wedding—"

"You're kidding. You were looking for a replacement?"

"Not really, but I did mention to Suzanne that if she knew anyone she wanted to make an honest man of . . ."

Matt started laughing and had trouble stopping. "You're the damnedest woman."

"I know it's crazy, but a woman who thinks she's lost the man she loves is a desperate person."

"Just say that last part again."

"A desperate person . . ."

"No, before that. The man she loves."

"Yes, I do love you, Matt. I wanted to tell you, but I didn't think I'd have the chance. I didn't think you felt the same."

"I just told you."

"I know, but I could hardly believe . . ."

"Believe, Molly." He threaded his fingers through her hair. "I love you. I love the way you look in the morning with your hair all tangled. I love the way you blush—a woman who can still blush is a treasure. I love the way you stand your ground and fight for your beliefs." He kissed her softly. "I love the way you look in that little red silky thing. I love how you fit into my home and my life. And most of all I love kissing you and making love to you."

"Then kiss me quick, Matt."

Matt covered her mouth with his, and they stood in the cold starlit night, arms wrapped around each other's bodies. His mouth was warm and hungry, and Molly opened to him like a flower. She remembered past kisses they'd shared, but this was more wonderful than all of them because it expressed the love they'd finally found in each other.

He took her hand and led her inside. The house was dark and Matt, one arm still around Molly, moved aside the fireplace screen and lit the fire. It roared up immediately, and they shed their jackets and pulled the sofa close. Molly settled in the curve of his arm and looked up into his eyes, eyes that had always surprised her by their color, somewhere between blue and gray. She'd probably never decide. But it didn't matter. They were the eyes of the man she loved.

"It's time for us to talk," Matt said, taking her hand. "First, about your job. It means a lot to you, doesn't it?"

"It does, but when we were on the porch, I remembered something Brent said. He told me that in a way he felt free now, and I guess I feel that way, too. Maybe losing my job wouldn't be the worst thing in the world."

"I think it would be great."

"I know. You're not fond of *Wedding*."

"Actually, I don't care about the magazine one way or the other. All I care about is you. If you're not tied to a desk, you can travel with me. There're some wonderful places I'd like to show you, Molly. I don't want to see them by myself anymore. I don't want to be alone. I want you with me." He pulled her close.

"I'm not sure I'd be a very good travel companion. I've never camped out. I don't know anything about living in a tent, and wildlife makes me very nervous."

Matt laughed. "Even towns in Tibet and Nepal have hotels, Molly. I promise you won't be living in a tent on the side of Mount Everest."

"But what would I do while you climb mountains?"

"Shop, take pictures—"

"Okay, that'll occupy the first day. Then what? I've worked all my life, Matt."

"Then explore wedding customs in strange places. You should see the rituals in India and Pakistan. They're exotic and colorful and fascinating. They'd make great copy."

"Weddings around the world." Molly thought for a moment. "I love the idea. Maybe it's the way to make things right with the magazine. Give them such a great idea they can't say no, and if they do, I'll bet another magazine would go for it."

"You know what we're talking about, Molly?"

"Yes, traveling and writing and—"

"Molly." Matt turned her toward him, putting his hands under her sweater and caressing her skin, which had been warmed both by the fire and his nearness.

"We're talking about a wedding. We're talking about you and me getting married." His words caressed her just as his hands did. "I want to marry you."

Molly thought her heart would burst with joy. She took a deep, trembling breath. "And I—"

"Yes, Molly? Tell me." He kissed her, again and again, and even if she'd been able to answer, his lips prevented it. Finally he pulled away and looked down at her. "What do you want, Molly?"

"I want to marry you, too."

"At last, we agree on something."

"From now on we'll agree a lot more often—maybe," she added and they both laughed with glee. Married. She was going to be married to Matt Kincaid. "When? We'll need time—"

"How about the day after tomorrow?" Matt asked casually. "I hear there's an open slot. I hear a caterer's been hired and someone's baked a cake."

"You mean here? Now? Krista's wedding?"

"Not Krista's wedding. Our wedding, yours and mine. We'll just use Krista's trappings."

"It's not possible. I mean, how could we—"

"No more arguing, Molly. You said you needed a replacement wedding. So here we are. You'll figure out the rest. You're the expert," he said confidently.

The idea was wild and impossible and the most exciting thing Molly had ever heard. Her mind went into overdrive. "We'll need a license and blood tests. There's no way we'd have time."

He kissed her again, so hard she not only stopped talking, she stopped thinking.

For a long time they devoted themselves to the kiss. Then Matt stopped long enough to remind her, "Trust me, Molly. One of the perks of being a local celebrity is that I can arrange things. I know the judge, I know someone at the license bureau. With my connections and your expertise, we can handle it."

She looked up at him, not really believing what was happening. "We're really going to do this, aren't we?"

"Molly, we're going to have the best damned wedding that Dillard, Colorado, has ever seen."

"HOLD STILL, MOLLY. Quit squirming." Suzanne was sitting on the floor, bracelets jangling as she hemmed up the last section of the wedding dress. "I don't know how I got talked into this. We should've had a real seamstress."

"There wasn't time," Molly reminded her.

"Well, I just hope this holds."

"Don't worry, it will. Thanks, Suzanne," Molly said as she helped her off the floor. "Now it's time for you to get dressed in that hot pink outfit."

"Not yet." Suzanne began bustling around until she found what she was looking for. "Here, this is for you," she said, holding out a small box.

Molly opened it. "Pearl earrings. Oh, Suzanne, they're lovely."

"Just right for your dress. They're not antiques by any means, but I think they can fit into the wedding tradition of something old. Lord knows I'm old, and I wore them years ago. Put them on."

Molly did as she was told, but something nagged at her mind. "Were these for—"

"Krista. Yes, they were, but now they're for you and don't you say a word about it."

Molly gave Suzanne a hug. "You and Brent have been so great. I never could have pulled this off without you."

"It's been good for us, too," Suzanne said. "Kept our minds off Krista and gave us a reason to celebrate. And this is going to be a marvelous party." She threw open the door. "Come on in, ladies."

Suzanne disappeared to get dressed as the bridesmaids floated in like shimmering clouds of lilac. They were followed by Judi Linquist, who'd shown up on schedule to shoot the wedding—only to find a different bride and groom.

"Those dresses look beautiful on all of you," Molly told them.

"I think we look like a covey of Victorian maidens," Alison replied as she executed a little pirouette. "But we're not here to show off. We've come to finish your little ceremony. Something old . . ."

"Something new . . ." Diane stepped forward, holding out her hand. "A new penny. You have to put it in your shoe."

"We don't know what it means," Lisa added, "but it's a wedding tradition, isn't it?"

"Lisa, you're such an airhead," Diane said, rolling her eyes. "Of course, it's a tradition. How's it feel, Molly?"

"Can't feel a thing." She wiggled her toes and took a step as the camera flashed.

"Now for something borrowed," Alison said. "Everyone knows that I had kind of a crush on Matt myself for about—oh, ten years or so." Molly joined the other two girls in laughter. "That's why I think it's appropriate for this to be from me." She held out a gold heart on a delicate chain. "It won't show under your dress, but you'll know it's there. I've always worn it on important occasions." She fastened the chain around Molly's neck.

Molly felt her eyes brim over with tears. "I knew that was going to happen," she complained. "I knew I would cry."

"Don't worry. This'll stop the tears," Lisa said, holding up a lacy blue garter. "It's from my boyfriend's fraternity. I got it at the last dance so it's also old and borrowed as well as blue so it would've fit all the categories."

"Lisa," Alison interrupted, "we don't have time for the explanation. Molly has to get married today, remember? Just make the presentation."

"All right." Lisa held out the garter, which Molly slipped on, holding on to Alison and Diane for balance.

"This is going to be the best photo yet," Alison announced. "Smile everyone."

"Show more leg, Molly," Lisa directed.

As the camera snapped, Molly felt the tears brimming up again. "Now I'm really going to cry. You've all been so wonderful, helping me out, agreeing to be in my wedding."

"We wouldn't have missed it for anything," Alison told her.

"We get these beautiful dresses," Diane chimed in.

"And we'll be in *Wedding* magazine," Lisa finished. "Krista was crazy to pass that up. Does she know?"

"She called last night. They were somewhere in Mexico and heading farther south," Molly said, collapsing in a chair.

"What did she say?" Lisa asked. "I bet she freaked out."

Molly laughed. "More or less. She and Pete were both yelling and screaming. They're very happy for us." Molly felt the urge to cry again.

Alison quickly stepped over to her. "You'll smear your makeup. Besides, it's time for us to get the veil on you."

Molly sat still while the three bridesmaids pulled her hair away from her face, piled it on top of her head and put the veil in place. Then they turned her toward the mirror.

She was framed in the glass like a painting from the Victorian age. The dress seemed to suit her perfectly, as if she'd actually stepped out of the nineteenth century. Molly could hardly believe her eyes.

"You look beautiful," someone said, and Molly smiled back at her reflection. The dress was shimmering white, gleaming with seed pearls and sequins. The veil cascaded down her back, trailing to the floor in a waterfall of white lace.

"Me . . . a bride. I'm getting married," she said with wonder.

"In about three minutes," Alison warned. "Come on, ladies, we need one final makeup-and-hair check."

Each of the bridesmaids hugged Molly gingerly, careful not to wrinkle her dress.

"See you downstairs," Lisa called over her shoulder. "And don't forget to throw the bouquet my way."

The room was suddenly too quiet and empty. Molly continued staring into the mirror, trying to absorb that the wedding day was here at last—and it was *her* day. The final arrangements had been so hectic, she'd had little time to herself. Her mother and sister had dropped everything to take the trip to Colorado and their arrival had created a flurry of activity. The editor of *Wedding* had been charmed by the idea of a last-minute wedding, and she and Jeri had flown out, arriving just that morning amid a huge fanfare. It was hard to fathom that in a few minutes, she and Matt—

Molly heard footsteps on the stairs, and Brent burst into the room, resplendent in his morning coat and dark gray trousers. "I'm here to give away the bride. It's nearly time."

Molly's hands were shaking when she took her bouquet from the green tissues in the florist box. Brent gave her an encouraging smile, grabbed her hand and led her to the door. The harpist began to play, and the bridesmaids started down the stairs. Molly's heart beat so loudly that she could hardly hear the music.

"Is Matt here?"

Brent smiled down at her. "Of course, he's here."

"Does he seem nervous? Is he shaking?"

Brent took her hand. "I guarantee he's not as nervous as you. I thought you were an old pro at this, Molly."

"It was easy to be calm at someone else's wedding. This is mine!" she exclaimed.

"It sure is. And there's the wedding march. Show time, Molly!" He held out his arm.

THE REST WAS like a dream for Molly. She seemed to move in slow motion through waves of sound and light, not walking down the stairs but floating, not moving in time to the music but waltzing on air. Bright sunshine streamed through the skylight. The rooms were banked with spring flowers. She didn't really see them as they moved down the stairs, but the delicate fragrance was everywhere, sweeter than any perfume.

As they neared the bottom of the stairs, she saw Matt. Her heart was so full she thought it would burst. He stood tall and strong in his formal clothes, the sun gilding his hair. She couldn't hold back the tears when he smiled at her, his face lit up with love. Slowly, she and Brent began to walk toward Matt in the cadence of the music.

Then Matt did something that surprised her, something wedding protocol never advised. He left the side of the justice of the peace and the flower-laden altar and strode down the aisle toward Molly.

She imagined that everyone in the room was as shocked as she, but Molly didn't look at anyone else. All she saw was the man she loved coming toward her.

Matt knew he couldn't have waited another moment. He had to hold her now and let her know how much he loved her—now. He saw the look of joy on her face and the tears in her eyes, knowing that the intensity of his own emotions matched hers. Somehow, in all the confusion of life, in all the jumble of the modern world, he and Molly had managed to find each other, and if he had his way, they'd spend the rest of their lives together.

Matt reached for her, and Molly clung to him for a long moment. He bent down and kissed her and then whispered in her ear, "I love you, Molly."

"I love you, Matt. More than anything."

Together they started back up the aisle as the guests spontaneously rose to their feet and began to applaud.

Molly blinked back her tears and smiled, looking up at Matt in delight.

"Well, what do you expect, Molly? After all, isn't this the wedding of the year?"

THREE UNFORGETTABLE HEROINES
THREE AWARD-WINNING AUTHORS

Untamed

MAVERICK HEARTS

A unique collection of historical short stories that capture the spirit of America's last frontier.

HEATHER GRAHAM POZZESSERE—over 10 million copies of her books in print worldwide
Lonesome Rider—The story of an Eastern widow and the renegade half-breed who becomes her protector.

PATRICIA POTTER—an author whose books are consistently Waldenbooks bestsellers
Against the Wind—Two people, battered by heartache, prove that love can heal all.

JOAN JOHNSTON—award-winning Western historical author with 17 books to her credit
One Simple Wish—A woman with a past discovers that dreams really do come true.

Join us for an exciting journey West with
UNTAMED
Available in July, wherever Harlequin books are sold.

MAV93

LIGHTS, CAMERA, ACTION!

Hollywood Dynasty

HARLEQUIN®
Temptation

The Kingstons are Hollywood—two generations of box-office legends in front of and behind the cameras. In this fast-paced world egos compete for the spotlight and intimate secrets make tabloid headlines. Gage—the cinematographer, Pierce—the actor and Claire—the producer struggle for success in an unpredictable business where a single film can make or break you.

By the time the credits roll, will they discover that the ultimate challenge is far more personal? Share the behind-the-scenes dreams and dramas in this blockbuster miniseries by Candace Schuler!

THE OTHER WOMAN, #451 (July 1993)
JUST ANOTHER PRETTY FACE, #459 (September 1993)
THE RIGHT DIRECTION, #467 (November 1993)

Coming soon to your favorite retail outlet.

New York Times Bestselling Author

Sandra Brown

Tomorrow's Promise

She cherished the memory of love but was consumed by a new passion too fierce to ignore.

For Keely Preston, the memory of her husband Mark has been frozen in time since the day he was listed as missing in action. And now, twelve years later, twenty-six men listed as MIA have been found.

Keely's torn between hope for Mark and despair for herself. Because now, after all the years of waiting, she has met another man!

Don't miss TOMORROW'S PROMISE by SANDRA BROWN.

Available in June wherever Harlequin books are sold.

TP

Relive the romance...
Harlequin and Silhouette
are proud to present

by Request

A program of collections of three complete novels by the most
requested authors with the most requested themes. Be sure to
look for one volume each month with three complete novels by
top name authors.

In June: **NINE MONTHS** Penny Jordan
                        Stella Cameron
                        Janice Kaiser

**Three women pregnant and alone. But a lot can
happen in nine months!**

In July: **DADDY'S**   Kristin James
         HOME   Naomi Horton
                        Mary Lynn Baxter

**Daddy's Home... and his presence is long
overdue!**

In August: **FORGOTTEN** Barbara Kaye
           PAST   Pamela Browning
                         Nancy Martin

**Do you dare to create a future if you've forgotten
the past?**

Available at your favorite retail outlet.

◇ HARLEQUIN   ❤ *Silhouette*